ESCAPES

ESCAPES

Darian Diachok

Palmetto Publishing Group
Charleston, SC

Escapes
Copyright © 2018 by Darian Diachok
All rights reserved

First Edition

Printed in the United States

ISBN-13: 978-1-64111-176-8
ISBN-10: 1-64111-176-3

BOOK 1

BORDER SHIFTS IN POLAND AND THE SOVIET UNION RESULTING FROM WORLD WAR II
As Communism expanded westward, Poland and Germany contracted – demarcations approximate

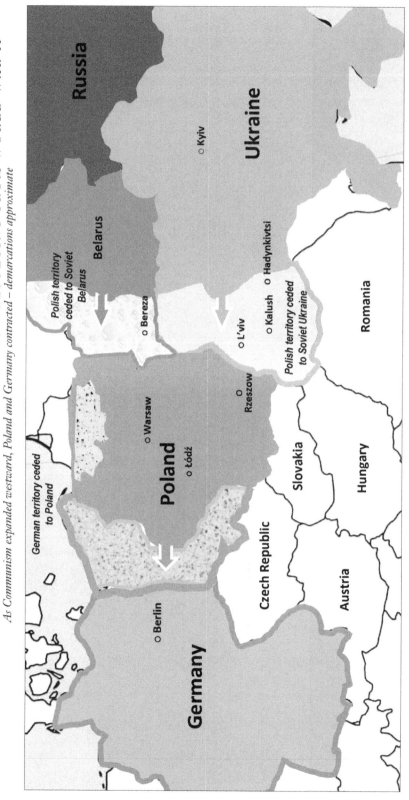

PROLOG TO THE STORM

People often reveal their true characters in spontaneous, unguarded moments. In his boyhood, the future dictator of the Soviet Union, Joseph Stalin, would celebrate successfully putting a practical joke over on one of his siblings by jumping up and down on one foot and snapping his fingers in triumph, his eyes shut in ecstasy. In school, he played the role of model student—homework done, lessons memorized—but behind the teacher's back, the young rebel played the wickedest tricks; getting his classmates into trouble, but staying clear of the teacher's suspicions. His saintly mother saw only her son's studious, creative side, and stretched the truth to get her young mischief-maker into Orthodox Christian seminary.

As a seminarian, Joseph quickly lost interest in theology, especially after discovering the atheistic, progressive works of Karl Marx, then circulating clandestinely as far as his native Georgia at the outskirts of Europe. The prospect of destroying the old order, upending religion, and thoroughly restructuring society captured him then and forever.

Now, thirty-five years later, as the new dictator of the Soviet Union, Joseph Stalin had amassed a growing array of enemies bent on revenge, and had to carefully map out alternate routes from his Kremlin office to his personal hideaway in Moscow's forested outskirts. Intent on an evening of seclusion, or on one of his vodka-swilling parties with his captive Politburo, he always chose the route himself, just as his chauffeur pulled out. Although Stalin had ridden to power posing as the most jovial of colleagues—a jokester and a soulmate to pour out your heart to—he had in fact perfected the art of leading his power-hungry Kremlin competitors to their own destruction. He had purged his new Politburo by first turning one half against the other, and soon after, by choosing new members who he would in turn set against the surviving Politburo members. Tonight, though, with the future of Europe at stake, Stalin stayed on in the Kremlin—sober as a lion tamer.

A thousand miles away in the German Alps, the stunning views of the Obersalzberg Mountains had always invigorated the new German dictator, a hypochondriac and lover of stirring Wagnerian opera. His best friend in his youth, Kubizek, had observed how totally transfixed young Adolph would remain after a performance of one of Wagner's *Ring of the Niebelung*, an epic saga of Norse gods, filled with betrayal, tragedy, and finally, redemption and heroic death. After staring out at the night sky, young Hitler would finally manage to say that the opera's message, its revelations, would one day lead him and his people to their true destiny.

And now thirty-five years later, as Chancellor of the Third German Reich, Hitler had just dispatched Foreign Minister Joachim von Ribbentrop to Moscow to negotiate a pact, a pact fraught with opportunity, but also with the greatest peril—a pact between mortal enemies. The two parties, Communist Russia and National Socialist Germany, had in fact earlier sworn to fight to the death.

Years earlier, Hitler had also destroyed his political competitors on the so-called Night of the Long Knives—just as Stalin had done. So with Stalin, Hitler knew he was dealing with a kindred spirit.

Hitler's feelers for possible cooperation presented Stalin with an opportunity of giddying proportions—an opportunity to relaunch the spread of Communism westward—and to trap the German dictator in his own designs. As Stalin knew only too well, the Communist Revolution of 1917, once destined to "spread like a prairie fire" and conquer the world, had failed to expand beyond the boundaries of the old Russian Empire. German World War I veterans, returning defeated but still superbly organized, had crushed a second planned Communist Revolution in Germany. For twenty years, Communism could spread no further. But Communist ideologues knew that nothing spread revolution quicker than more war. Stalin would give Hitler whatever he needed to make war possible—to provoke England and France into war against Germany in another world war.

Stalin knew that London and Paris had guaranteed Poland's security against any German aggression, and that Hitler was chafing at the bit to attack Poland. In fact, Hitler was only hesitating precisely because he feared another two-front war: Germany caught again between the Western Allies and Russia. Well, if that's all that prevented Hitler from starting another war, why not give him what he needed, a guarantee of Russia's neutrality? Behind the Kremlin's closed doors, Stalin confided to his inner circle that such a war, once successfully provoked, would at last destabilize western Europe, and after Germany, France, and England had bled themselves white in the trenches again, Stalin would march in as liberator, and finally impose Communism on the rest of Europe—as destiny demanded.

Hitler was even sweetening the pot by promising to divide up Poland with Russia. And if that wasn't enough, he'd let Stalin help himself to as much of eastern European land lying between them as he wanted.

Was the German subterfuge too obvious, a deal too good to be true? And was Stalin in turn fashioning a trap for him, too, just as he had for so many other rivals? Hitler and his entourage of fashionable celebrities awaited the results of the negotiations on the calm summer evening of August 28, 1939. The phone call came through. The chatter immediately ceased on the spacious terrace overlooking the stunning Alps, as if everyone recognized by Hitler's demeanor that Stalin had managed to put a gun to his head. Hitler blinked and finally assented. Ribbentrop returned to the negotiating table in the Kremlin to announce, "Der Führer stimmt der Unterzeichnung des Protocolls zu" (The Führer agrees to the signing of the Protocol).

As the entourage awaited confirmation from Moscow, clouds gathered at the Obersalzberg. One by one, the drinking glasses lowered as the sky began turning red, then an unearthly piercing green, and finally, a sulfur gray, the cauldron rushing toward them, as the winds sprang to life, hissing as if possessed. The retreat manager, Robert Döring, described the spectacle as "frightening, terrible, cruel, beautiful." At last, a woman in a sequin gown stammered, "My, my Führer, this means no good. It means blood, blood . . . and again, blood, destruction, and terrible suffering."

Robert Döring recalled that the celestial phenomenon had also produced a tremor in the Führer's body. Before following his last guests off the terrace, a thoroughly unnerved Hitler finally managed to utter, "Well, if it must happen, let it be now!'

THEO STARED AT THE OUTSTRETCHED VIOLIN LIKE a medic at a severed limb.

6

"Maybe it's out of tune," Steffie said with a giggle, and licked her fingers, stained red sorting the morning haul of mountain berries. He took the instrument from her and gently laid it to rest, closed the case with two hard snaps, and stared out the cottage window at the Carpathian Mountains, blue, distant, and solitary. Earlier that day, she had barely suppressed her yawns when he'd read her Franko's most tender poetry, though during their courtship she had boasted of a love for literature, and even a passion for performing the classics. He tore his eyes from her half-clothed, tanned torso, and sensed that this unsettling physical attraction, this chemistry, could no longer bridge the growing chasm between them.

He wandered around the log-frame cottage with its vaulted ceiling—the luxury honeymoon suite—and absently clicked on the shoulder-high radio of polished spruce, twisting the dial, squealing and squawking across the stations, as if looking for a wise voice that would clearly advise him. He paused for a frenzied announcement in Polish about yet another damned border skirmish with Germany, and clicked it off.

He looked past her toward the window and recalled how, on the first day of their honeymoon, Steffie had strewn a line of breadcrumbs onto the windowsill. Then a few moments later, she had managed – ever so gingerly – to encircle an unsuspecting thrush in her cupped hands. She had carefully handed him the tiny, pulsating creature, which, for a few precious seconds, felt like an anxious, exposed human heart – the pulse of life, in his hands. It thrilled his own heart to watch the thrush flit away in a series of arcs and escape toward the forested hills. On releasing the bird though, he felt a sadness, as if his own sister had flown away.

"Theo, if music is so important to you," Steffie said, "You could teach me to play – if it will make you happy, or if you wanted to show me off to friends."

"Steffie, sweetheart, you're missing the point," he said and turned away.

"Theo, in my heart," she protested, "I'm an artist, too—but in my own way."

"An artist in your own way," he repeated. "No, it takes years of –"

"You'll see … one day you will." She sat next to him. "Theo, please" she pleaded, "Don't let a silly violin become more important than our love." As he wrested himself out of her embrace, she asked, "What are you doing to us?"

"Steffie, you can't just … just mislead others –"

The door banged loudly. Steffie quickly covered herself and clutched the religious medallion suspended from her neck.

"What the hell?!" Theo said. "Who is it?"

"Germany invaded Poland!" someone yelled from behind the door.

Theo squinted, trying to process the ugly words. "What?!" he yelled. "When?"

"Germany invaded Poland—this morning—hours ago!"

Throwing the door open, Theo recognized Steve Chernyk, smart in his corporal's uniform, unbuttoned at the top, sweat trickling onto his white undershirt. "I thought I recognized the voice!" Theo said. "How did you find me?"

"How?" Chernyk shook his head. "Don't even ask."

"Don't even ask, sir!" Theo corrected. "Address a commanding officer properly."

"P-Poland attacked Germany?" Steffie stammered. They both looked at her.

"No, just the opposite," Chernyk corrected, a nervous grin distorting his features. "Sorry for interrupting your honeymoon, sir!"

Chernyk glanced at Steffie, wide-eyed on the bed. "Your new orders!" he called out. "A truck's waiting for you by the gate and a troop train first thing in the morning." Chernyk gave an exaggerated salute and walked off.

Steffie watched Theo throw together his change of clothes and his soap and comb and brush. "A lot can happen at the front. At least give me something to remember you by," she said.

For a moment, her skin felt warm, hot, like an unattended stove against his hands. He glanced at his watch and threw his rucksack over his shoulder.

"It's cold. Cover yourself," he said and reached for the door – images of the battlefield carnage of his father's generation flashing in his mind.

"Theo," she said, "You do know I love you, don't you?"

He exhaled, searching for words until he heard the blast of the horn, "I know, Steffie," he said, "I know you do."

THE OUTBREAK

By late summer, Europe's two great socialisms had suspended their bitter propaganda campaigns against each other. Suddenly, no more anti-Nazi editorials in Pravda, Communism's flagship daily, and no more anti-Soviet films in German Kino. The two European superpowers had turned their attention to their dismemberment of Poland.

In August, the German press had begun preparing the public for war with Poland. Successive headlines of the *Neue Mannheimer Zeitung* had complained to its readership that "Poland Refuses to Negotiate with Germany"; and "Arrogant Poland Sees Herself a Great Power"; and finally, "Poland's Ethnic Oppression Must Finally Come to an End," suggesting that Germany had settled on a pretext to invade—to protect Poland's German-speaking minority.

In England, the headlines of the *North-Eastern Gazette* had immediately responded to the German press with a challenge: "Blunt Message from the Cabinet: WE WILL STAND BY POLAND!"

A week later, on September 1, 1939, the *Neue Mannheimer Zeitung* had finally called England's bluff: "The Struggle against Poland Has Finally Begun.' Later that same day, the *New York Times* headlines had reported: "German Army Attacks Poland; Cities Bombed; Port Blockaded; Danzig Is Accepted into Reich."

Dublin's *Daily Mail* had reported that "Poland Sends SOS to London," prompting editorial writers to speculate if England and France, Poland's treaty signatories guaranteeing her borders, would in fact come to her defense. Dailies across western Europe and the United States began announcing support for Poland, with England and France announcing full mobilization – springing the giant trap Stalin had hoped Germany would fall into.

MAYBE THE SKIES SEEMED TOO BLUE, OR THE MOUN-tain air too fresh, for this crowd to fully grasp it, Theo thought. The focused and disciplined German Army was marching toward them this very morning! Not suspecting that in five years he'd return to this very spot as an exhausted refugee, he hitched up his backpack and pushed his way through the crowds at the Ivano-Frankivsk station. The unseasonably warm sun seemed to be pulling the lines of freshly shaven boys in khaki uniforms right out through the windows toward girls offering them flower bouquets. The boys were demanding kisses while the girls flirted, Theo noticed, as if the train were off to some championship match. A trio of singing soldiers stepped in his path and hoisted up a bottle. "Boys," Theo quietly muttered, and pushed away the translucent liquid thrust in his face. "Don't you realize? It's Germans you're about to face!"

"Germans?" one soldier slurred in Polish, his eyes crossed. "Ha! They don't even ride real tanks—just cardboard mockups."

His comrade laughed and pointed a finger at an abandoned baby carriage. "Pop! You can knock each one out with a cork gun. This invasion, all bluff!"

Theo parried an attempted drunken embrace. "A bluff? Then why do you need that—that extra courage?" he demanded and knocked the bottle out of his hand. "Show respect for rank!" At twenty-seven, he was nearly ten years older than these enlisted recruits.

He forced his pack onto a car reserved for officers of the Twenty-Fourth Reserve Infantry Division, and pushed through the clogged corridor. A whistle cut through the babble of voices. The engines roared to life, as did his emotions. Didn't duplicity constitute grounds for annulment? the thought welled up.

He stared at the billowing steam engulfing the platform, and recalled his first sight of Steffie just four months ago. He had spotted her in a kaleidoscope of couples twirling to a waltz. He recalled dropping his violin to his side when he recognized her partner, that big talker, Chernyk. Feeling protective and thinking she deserved better, he had hurried off the stage, telling his mandolin player Panasevich to take over the lead. His four-man string combo heroically played on without losing a beat. Then he'd tapped Chernyk's shoulder. Chernyk lamely protested Theo "pulling rank," but Steffie deftly withdrew, and Theo took her to the center of the dancehall, where no one could cut in, and just like that, he held the exciting brunette in his arms. She not only looked like his first love, the woman who had just left him, nearly mortally wounding him, but she felt the same in his embrace, anticipating each step as if they'd been rehearsing all day, his embrace tightening, his pain releasing, until she'd pushed his shoulder back, and whispered, "Hey, hey, they stopped playing."

He opened his eyes and turned red, and despite the reams of poetry he'd once published, he couldn't conjure up a thing to say, as Steffie studied his darting eyes. "Do I somehow remind you of her, the other Steffie?" she'd asked.

"Ah, maybe that's it," he'd said, "You do look so much alike."

"A loss for her," she'd retorted, "and a gain for someone else, maybe someone more deserving."

"Well, I – I'm sorry. I should be getting back."

"No, please stay," she had said. "They can play a few numbers without you."

The chestnut trees were already blossoming that warm spring night, and he had wondered if his luck was about to change.

A couple had passed them on their way back in, the man short, collar outturned, the first two shirt buttons rakishly undone. His partner, in a tight roaring-twenties chemise, glanced at Theo—perhaps a little too long—and winked at Steffie.

"My sister, Zosia," Steffie explained. "She thinks she finally found somebody. But I'll let you in on a secret. She was always a little crazy about you, too."

Chernyk had overtaken them on the path, arm in arm with a new partner, a blonde this time. Chernyk had chuckled and advised Steffie against taking Theo's bait. The quiet ones, he'd warned, were the real schemers. The blonde laughed. Steffie took Theo's hand, her fingers fitting effortlessly into his, and turned off the path toward the lake. "Guys like Chernyk!" she'd said, "Give them a smile, a wink and a compliment, and they're in the bag – too easy! I'm looking for someone who can resist me – someone with character," she laughed. "Don't worry about him. Besides, I'm not even his type. He just doesn't know it yet."

Theo knew of Steffie's many suitors—even one of the famous Bandera brothers was courting her—and said, "I think you're probably everyone's type."

"Well, you might be, too," she'd said, and added that the girls in Kalush knew all about his breakup, and were just waiting in line for a chance at him. He'd lamely mumbled in reply that the first Steffie would be hard to replace, and even more lamely, that the two of them used to play violin duets.

"We have a saying in our family," Steffie had responded, as he regarded her in the semi-darkness. "To recover from a loss, you only need to knock the wedge out of your heart with a bigger wedge."

Maybe it was indeed that simple, he had thought. But he didn't explain that the violin duets with the first Steffie had bridged a gap he thought nothing could ever bridge with another woman, especially after a score of rejections. Through the trees, he remembered seeing rowboats in silhouette against the moon, and, as the oars came to life, the moonlight scouring the lake with widening silver ribbons. He'd studied the lake for a moment. "Look out there, Steffie," he'd whispered, "and tell me what you see."

Steffie took in the shimmering lake. "See that long band of silver?" she'd said, and pointed. "Out there at the very end of the lake? That's where all the silver ripples swim from—that's their home." She looked at him, and back at the lake. "And look! They're coming out to play now."

As two rowboats approached each other, the ripples multiplied. Theo and Steffie stood transfixed as the boats crossed paths, the ripples converting the water surface into two sparkling mazes that merged and unexpectedly disappeared, and a moment later reappeared in a brilliant new pattern.

"I've never seen anything like it," he'd said, and turned to her.

"Just a matter of taking the time to look," she'd said, and had raised her chin and closed her eyes.

He had resisted kissing her, and instead said, "I'd wanted to say that, that you dance beautifully—in fact, like dancing with a broom."

"Like a broom?" she'd responded, wide-eyed.

"No, no, I mean, you're easy to handle—uh, on the dancefloor," he backtracked, instantly regretting having turned down her kiss, and wondering if he'd ever get a second chance. "A compliment!" he explained. "And . . . supposedly, you're quite a teacher. I hear your kids love you. And, and I can see you have a whole horde of friends." She began to laugh, so he added, "Do you have any faults?"

Steffie had shook her head and laughed. "You mean, am I perfect?" she'd said. "Well, I *do* curse—no, I mean, *really* curse—sometimes like a sailor."

"That's not so bad," Theo had pressed on. "Tell me, what's the worst thing you've ever done? I used to steal and drink communion wine when I served as an altar boy. What could be worse?"

Steffie grimaced and looked away. He watched her stiffen, and in the reflected moonlight, he thought he saw tears welling up in her eyes.

"Please don't take me seriously," he'd begun. "I was just—"

"No"—Steffie sighed—"some things maybe . . . shouldn't stay hidden forever. Well, I've never told anyone this." She paused and straightened, her moonlit profile upright for a moment against the trembling waves. "But I still can't," she said at last, lowering her head. "It's too much."

"I didn't mean to open up such a . . . painful," Theo's voice trailed away as he watched the last rowboat retreating into the shadows. "Maybe we should go back," he said.

"Wait," Steffie said abruptly. "Please wait. If I don't tell someone, then I'll—" She paused. "You're absolutely the first to hear this—no one even in my family." She ran her fingers lightly across her face, and said, "When my little brother Romko was sick for his third day with dysentery, my father sent me for medicine. I was too embarrassed to say 'dysentery,' so you know what I told the druggist? I told him my brother needed something for a headache, and I came back home with nothing but . . . nothing but powdered aspirin."

Theo had whistled softly. "And Romko—" he began.

"Yes," Steffie had answered. "As he got worse, they gave him more . . . aspirin. Romko didn't survive the night." She turned toward Theo, searching his eyes. "How can I forgive myself?" she whispered, and turned away again. "You see, I can't."

Theo knew of Steffie's two strapping brothers, Slavko and Vlodko, but hadn't suspected a third one, long gone now. "You were just a child!" he whispered, and regarded the smooth nape of her naked neck. "What a burden to carry," he added, but resisted a second impulse to embrace her, to somehow grant her absolution—the first moment that marriage had entered his mind.

The train shrieked a final warning. Theo looked out at the crowds at the station, imagining Steffie running to breathlessly promise to master some musical instrument for him.

A hand steadied him as the train lurched forward.

"So, you fled your love nest just to defend Mother Poland?" Theo heard the jest in Ukrainian behind him. "Well, you won't find her in all that smoke." Theo turned and beheld the unmistakable toothy grin— Panasevich, as defiant as ever, his rogatywka field cap pushed rakishly forward, the moustache freshly trimmed, the forehead lumpy from a soccer kick, another Ukrainian in Polish uniform.

Finally feeling connected, Theo grabbed him by the shoulders, remembering that cold spring day in Polish officer candidate school. He'd been struggling to rise from a kick to the side, when Panasevich had winked from the punishment formation marching by, the wink and that tilted cap giving Theo just enough support to survive another bout with that sadistic drill instructor. With two weeks left in candidate school, the lowbrow Pole had zeroed in on him as his next target, after having harassed and driven another educated Ukrainian officer candidate to suicide.

Theo knew Panasevich hated open displays of gratitude. "I guess our colonels couldn't bluff their way out of this one," Theo said.

Panasevich nodded and leaned his Mauser 98 rifle against the cabin corner and loosened his field belt, sagging with trios of leather-bound ammunition packs. "Oh no, Poland's become too great a superpower to negotiate with Germany!" He snorted and dropped the belt onto the seat. He sat back and spread back his arms. "Why bother honoring an actual plebiscite, right? Who cares that the entire Danzig Corridor wanted to reunite to Germany."

Theo tightened the yellow cover on his gas mask. "Plebiscites," he said with a yank. "What about when our own people voted for independence from Poland twenty years ago? Ah! The will of the people." He grimaced. "Democracy? Panko, governments only listen to the people—"

"When it serves their own damned interests! Don't lecture me," Panasevich concluded. "I never thought it would come to this either." He carefully pulled his bayonet out of its scabbard and slowly turned the blade. Both men stared at the gleaming steel until Panasevich shoved it back and quickly leaned forward. "And what about *our* independence?" he whispered.

Theo stood and looked out the window at the lines of refugees along the tracks walking in the opposite direction. "You're dreaming, Panko," he whispered. A line of trees moved into view to block the sun as the train slowed at another station. "Our day will come," Theo said, "but today—*today*—we're Polish officers . . . and we're about to be tested."

Panasevich pulled a pack of cigarettes from his tunic pocket. "Tested?" He chuckled and tore off the wrapping. "Hell, our generals believe they'll be parading in Berlin in three weeks, right on the damned Kurfürstendamm!"

Two high-ranking Polish officers stepped behind him into the compartment, as Panasevich held a flame to the cigarette dangling from his lips and mumbled, "Hell, we're just reservists. We won't see any action."

Theo recognized a captain and a major, both cavalry officers, and declined Panasevich's cigarette. "I'm not so sure," Theo murmured, and stood and saluted, two fingers bent to his cap—God and country.

The major ignored the two lieutenants and turned toward the overhead bin. "Captain," he said, "why are these two officers speaking in a backward peasant dialect?"

The captain pulled off his cap, revealing an uncommonly high forehead. He glanced back and forth between the pair. "I don't know, sir, why anyone with higher learning would prefer a peasant dialect," he replied matter-of-factly.

The major turned to reveal a square, brown moustache amid a chunky but noble face, a bit like the British comedian, Oliver Hardy. Two elaborate medals from previous campaigns garnished his chest. "Don't officers represent the pride of Poland?" he asked no one in particular. Theo glanced down at his boots smeared with grass blades, for a moment, feeling naked.

"Peasant *dialect*?" Panasevich repeated, starting to rise, but Theo grabbed his sleeve and pulled him back. Theo had instantly recognized the major's accent. "We don't all have the good fortune to come from Warsaw," Theo observed. Before the major could respond, he added, "Any news on the disposition of the German Army?"

The captain grimaced and examined his hands as if he could find the answer in his fingernails.

Panasevich leaned forward. "Yes," he said. "What exactly justifies all this confidence?"

The major looked back and forth between the two lieutenants and decided to reply. "It's true," he said, "we are outnumbered—but only on paper. I estimate we're fielding a little over half a million men against perhaps several million Germans. But the Germans can't attack us with their whole army. They have to leave half their forces behind to protect their border with France. And France is our ally. If they come with half their army, we can stop them. If they come with their whole army, France will easily march right into Berlin. Their reckless gamble will turn into a historical mistake—the end of Hitler. Besides," he added with a wink, "our equipment is French—the latest."

Theo recalled young volunteers from his boyhood marching out of his town of Hadynkivtsi in the last war—their songs booming, their heads held high—and then the next week, the horses wearily pulling back the carts stacked with the dead like cordwood, bloodied relatives for families to claim. "So if I understand you, sir, our best odds are no better than two or three to one," Theo said.

The captain looked up, his eyes brimming with accusation. "The defenders always have the advantage," he said. "We'll do just fine."

"Yes," the major agreed, smoothing his moustache. "A Pole doesn't fear three-to-one odds. In 1920, we turned back the Russians at five-to-one odds. Gentlemen, I know. I was there."

Theo straightened up. "You fought at the Miracle on the Vistula?"

The major, his medals sparkling in the abrupt sunlight as the train curved northward into cultivated fields, said, "I'm sure the Reds considered us an easy obstacle. But we turned back an army five times our size."

"And blocked the Communist Revolution from crossing into western Europe," Theo added.

"Pilsudski," the captain added, "an amateur, but a military genius. Without Pilsudski, Poland would—"

The doors swung open with a bang as the train pitched to a halt. A whiff of fertilizer invaded the compartment, overwhelming the cigarette smoke from the aisles. Theo grabbed his Mauser and yanked the door open, and jumped down onto the track ballast, his boots dislodging a few rocks with the extra weight of his gear. Khaki uniforms began filling the curved space along the train tracks. Panasevich appeared at his side as a messenger ran toward the major.

"German Stukas—"

"What?"

"Stukas, Stukas! Dive bombers—they wrecked an armored train up ahead. We can't get through! You'll have to form up and march out to your rendezvous points," the messenger concluded.

As the major unfolded a map, Panasevich volunteered a last remark. "You must know," he said, "that the Ukrainians fought on Pilsudski's side in that battle."

The major looked at Panasevich uncomprehendingly.

"He means Petliura's army," Theo explained.

"Petliura?" the major asked, looking out excitedly at the lines of men assembling along the tracks.

"Petliura," Panasevich repeated. "The greatest Ukrainian general of this generation."

"Ah, Ukrainians!" the major uttered. "This time, we'll do it alone."

The reservists massed in the farm fields, each lieutenant to a platoon, each captain to a company. Theo looked at his charges—about thirty recruits, probably half Polish, half Ukrainian, solemn faces, pimply faces, strong peasant faces, some in crested French helmets, others in field caps—looking to him for protection, for leadership. He felt the wooden stock against his back, his Mauser just a hornet, he thought, against a swarm of locusts gathering somewhere. Someone would have to tell his men how to handle the grenades being passed out, supposedly innovative and lethal, a new Polish design. He looked at his pulsing right hand—the veins still obedient to his beating heart—and gripped the rifle strap, vowing to himself that he would bring his men back alive.

 A WEEK INTO THE INVASION, THE POLISH High Command debated if their original battle plan could still work against the German invaders. The Polish Inspectorate had identified weaknesses in the infantry and air force earlier in the year, and had concluded that, without military treaties, Poland could not successfully defend her borders. In case of war, the Poles would have to count on English and French guarantees to come to their rescue. But the Poles could hold out for two weeks by blunting—not stopping—an initial German invasion, and then relying on hit-and-run guerilla tactics, waiting until the estimated seventy French divisions mobilized and crossed the border to take on the German Army.

But even blunting the German onslaught was proving difficult. Poland's thinly spread lines of defense along the entire frontier with Germany presented the ideal target for Germany's new blitzkrieg style of warfare. Within the first week, Germany's tank brigades, under the pioneering military tactician Heinz Guderian, had broken through the northern defenses. In the south, another attack was mauling the famed Krakow army—the two campaigns clearing the way to a desperately defended Warsaw.

At this point, the German Foreign Ministry asked Moscow why the Red Army hadn't attacked Poland yet, from the east, as agreed. Stalin dallied, preferring for Germany to bear the military cost of the invasion, and waiting for Germany to take full international opprobrium for invading a sovereign country. The German Foreign Ministry replied that Germany was now considering establishing an independent Ukrainian state out of the territory that Russia was supposed to seize. The threat hit home. Ten days later, Stalin followed up on his agreement and invaded from the east—taking eastern Poland nearly unopposed.

AN ORDER ECHOED DOWN ALONG THE LINES: "NO drinking from canteens under pain of court martial." Theo, a committed teetotaler after a nearly disastrous bout with the bottle at nineteen, knew thirst would be tormenting the soldiers after their boozy send-offs. Well, at some point they'd have to learn. He studied the lines of sacrificial lambs; reservists, all, their rifles obediently tilted across their shoulders at forty-five degrees. At least they got that right from their weekend drills.

The Twenty-Fourth Reserve Infantry Division moved out into the open countryside in double columns, the horses pulling iron-wheeled supply carts over the dirt roads that bisected the quiet Polish fields. He wondered if his green boys could deploy those mortars and heavy guns strapped to the rattling carts in time to counter any real ambush. For an instant, he wished he could dissolve into those lovely hibernating fields. He had become a reserve officer to improve his miserable Ukrainian life, not to die for Poland, or worse, to return a cripple.

Gray silhouettes of farmhouses began protruding from the early morning haze. A brunette, much like Steffie, ran to the fence, shouting "Poland Lives!" Her family waved as they marched through their dark-brown farmland. *Land*, Theo thought—the very reason he'd finagled his way into their army. The Polish government was granting its military officers land in overcrowded western Ukraine, good farming land. Theo's father had in fact left the family to work the new Canadian Pacific Railroad, to earn enough Canadian dollars to return and buy a few acres. When World War I erupted, Canada had frozen the bank accounts of its eastern European workers, who technically, now came from enemy lands. His father had returned empty-handed after ten long years. And now Theo was trying another path.

No, Poland wasn't making it easy for Ukrainians. He thought of the Wozniaks, the family he had just married into, and his three new brothers-in-law. Slavko Wozniak, the eldest, was spending his career in endless court battles trying to outmaneuver Polish economic restrictions against homegrown Ukrainian dairy cooperatives. Slavko's younger brother, Vlodko, had accepted Holy Orders during a government crusade against the Ukrainian Catholic Church. But Viktor Sabat, Zosia's husband and Theo's youngest and smallest brother-in-law, at five feet six, had reacted the most emotionally of the three—direct confrontation. Viktor had joined the outlawed Ukrainian Organization of Nationalists, which was waging a guerrilla war against the Polish government. Viktor's rebellion had led to a string of prison terms. In fact, Viktor was doing time at that very moment in Bereza, Poland's harshest prison.

Theo worried how these three defiant Ukrainians regarded him, a fellow Ukrainian in Polish uniform. He wondered if any of them suspected the tortuous politics, the strings he had had to pull to finagle a spot in officer candidate school. Sure, the Pilsudski's government had set aside five percent for non-Polish minorities in the Polish Officer Corps, for strictly the best and the brightest non-Poles. But the Polish brass, nationalistic to the core, didn't like it one bit, and gave their drill sergeants free reign to unleash any cruelties they could think of against Ukrainian candidates like him and Panasevich. And not everyone could survive their gauntlets to earn a commission. But besides that? Besides having refused to quit, Theo had had to admit to his own nationalistic stirrings, a burning inside to refute, once and all, the motto that Poles were born to lead, and Ukrainians, born to follow.

"Is it true German machine guns fire fifteen hundred rounds a minute?" asked a Polish reservist, interrupting Theo's thoughts.

Theo turned to a scrawny young man in glasses, marching out of step. "Soldier, that rate of fire would be what? Three times ours," he said, hoping to sound convincing, convincing enough to relieve the soldier's apparent fear of combat, of death. "Impossible! Just a rumor!"

POLES LIKED TO CALL THEIR COUNTRY the "Christ of Nations," some would say for good reason. In the seventeenth century, a Polish army came to the rescue of the Austrians to stop another massive Islamic invasion of Europe. Their combined armies defeated the Turkish army at Vienna and saved Christendom.

But in the next century, history turned a new page: The French Revolution of 1789 vowed to replace the old feudal hierarchy of privileged lords and lowly serfs with a new order of "all citizens equal under the law." Poland supported this seismic political shift, and had again dispatched armies to buttress the French Revolution. Poland's actions alarmed her powerful neighbors—Russia, Prussia, and Austria, Europe's timeless feudal empires—who wanted no revolutionary ideas inflaming their serfs. The three monarchies combined to defeat and partition this upstart in their midst, and for five generations, Poland vanished from Europe's map. But all three monarchies collapsed in the First World War, themselves never to reappear on Europe's maps. Playing her cards deftly at the Versailles Treaty to reorganize Europe, Poland emerged from the ruins of World War I fully independent—an astonishing political resurrection for this Christ of Nations

At the Versailles Conference, France saw to it that Poland got extra territory—parts of Germany's eastern provinces, with millions of ethnic Germans, along with the Austrian province of Galicia, with its millions of Ukrainians. But this geographic expansion came with a price. Poles had to keep a constant, wary eye on the ethnic Germans, and another eye on the ethnic Ukrainians.

While Poles set to work rebuilding their country, most western Ukrainians adapted to the new masters, dropping German to learn Polish. Their previous masters, the Austrians, had let Ukrainians build their own schools and churches, and compete for jobs. The Versailles Treaty expected the new Polish government to treat her new minorities just as fairly. But radical Ukrainians had long chafed under foreign rule, and quickly fomented insurrections against Polish rule. In retaliation, Poland closed down Ukrainian higher education, shut down schools, burned scores of churches, and kept Ukrainians out of the work force unless they discarded their Ukrainian identity and "Polonized." And perhaps most provocatively, the new Polish government drove thousands of western Ukrainians out of their ancestral lands and brought in Polish settlers.

This uneasy ethnic mix of Poles and Ukrainians—this newest version of the Christ of Nations—faced another severe test.

"COLUMN, LEFT!" BY MIDAFTERNOON, THE FATIGUED men of the Twenty-Fourth Reserve Infantry Division finally set their boots onto the Rzeszow highway, tree-lined and shaded, but did not once see a hint of the enemy. They reformed into units, four across, the lieutenants, front right. Whistles blew, and the men stepped aside. A cavalry unit clattered past, noisy against the pavement, triangular banners flying, their spirited Arabians carrying slender riders in dashing uniforms. *Costume-ball uniforms,* Theo thought, *from an era when Poles believed themselves anointed to spread chivalry through the world.* How long would any exposed cavalry, no matter how well tailored, last against those rumored fifteen hundred rounds a minute?

They marched their twentieth straight hour right into the town of Rzeszow, where schoolgirls in blue coats, with pretty, matching bonnets waved little red-and-white flags from the sidewalks, and Roman Catholic priests flung holy water. He scanned the sky for planes in between the rooftops. He'd yet to see his first single-wing plane, but heard the new German fighters made Polish biplanes look like they were standing still; darting demons, impossible targets for infantry rifles.

"Sir," the young reservist at Theo's side said, "can we rest? Blisters!"

His own right foot pulsing with razor-like pain, Theo managed to say, "Ignore the pain. They'll pop."

Another order rolled down—quick march. *A bad sign*, Theo thought, rushing these untested men to plug some gap in the front. They quick marched on into the night's cool embrace. A brook meandered close by, like a hunting dog keeping them company well past midnight; the music of water over the stones harmonizing with the pounding of boots, the pounding of boots, the pounding . . . until Theo drifted off into deep sleep.

All at once, he became aware of an engine droning above him and blinked his eyes open. He'd slept while marching, right into daylight, and came to a split-second halt without breaking formation. Was it possible? As if on cue, he raised his binoculars. "Double struts," he said. "One of ours!" The plane banked and glinted in the sunlight, a German cross marking its fuselage, a Swastika, its vertical stabilizer. "No," he corrected, "a Henschel!"

"Open fire!" the captain commanded, lowering his own binoculars. Spent shells clinked to the pavement around their boots, some soldiers shooting until their magazines emptied, while the reconnaissance plane banked again and drifted out of range. "Psa krew [dog's blood], they know our position," the captain muttered.

Sentries ran off to safeguard the perimeter while the major called headquarters. Panasevich limped over and collapsed next to Theo. "Creepy, isn't it?" he whispered. "Marching two days without seeing the enemy."

Theo looked at his boys, prostrate along the fence. "I know," he said. "Maybe they've been watching *us*."

Panasevich unstrapped his helmet. "I've made my peace," he said, pouring water onto a handkerchief and dousing the back of his head. "A German bullet's out there with my name on it—or it isn't—as long as I don't get my nuts shot off."

Theo unscrewed his canteen, recalling that third and fateful day of his honeymoon, that moment he had unlatched the black case and lifted the violin. He hated himself just as much now, as then, for putting Steffie through the test. What else could he do, but try to put to rest the growing suspicion.

He distinctively recalled plucking each violin string, turning the peg until the G-string creaked before plucking again—yes, all in tune. He had cradled his jaw over the worn chinrest, feeling the strings' stiffness against his arched fingers, the fine balance, and the precision of the bow in his right hand. He'd come to think that his left hand subdued the instrument, sort of tamed it; and the right—the right—seduced it, made it sing . . . or weep!

He'd pulled the bow, and the first note had reverberated through the cottage, filling it, owning it. "Ready," he'd said. "Play us something." Steffie had set aside the bowl, drying her fingers against the bed covers.

He watched her take the violin in her wrong hand, frown, reverse the bow and the violin, bowing theatrically; yes, by that time, he was getting used to her antics. She waved the bow in a circle and shut her eyes. The first note grated his ears. She stared wide-eyed at the strings. The second pull had screeched like a stung animal.

A bright light flashed to Theo's left, and then a raucous boom. The men jumped to their feet, and went for their rifles. "Stay put!" Theo yelled, and sprinted to Panasevich's unit. Two red stumps instantly caught his eye: a soldier, unconscious, with a broad, peasant face, handless arms thrown back, a severed hand a few meters from the prostrate soldier's boots.

The crowd stepped aside for the officers. A pair of medics ran in. One knelt; the other threw open his bag. "Is he alive?" Panasevich asked.

"See that blood pulsing from his wrists?" the first medic said. "But he will die, sir, and soon, if we don't stop that bleeding."

"What happened?" Panasevich asked a soldier kneeling at the casualty's side.

"Uh, we, we were resting, sir, chatting," the young soldier stammered. "He was rolling one of those new grenades from hand to hand..."

"What do you want us to do with this, sir?" Theo heard, and turned to see a corporal holding the other severed hand, with the marriage ring surprisingly still in place. "Must have sailed a good twenty-five meters," the corporal said. "Need it? Or . . . or should I bury it?"

The casualty's friend stood up and retched. As the junior medic busied himself tearing lengthy strips of gauze, Panasevich looked to the senior medic for guidance, who shrugged and said, "I really don't know, sir. Right now, I need help pinching these arteries shut."

"Go help him," Panasevich ordered the casualty's friend. "You need to get used to it."

Theo watched the pair pull out and tie off the pulsing arteries, while the junior medic washed off the stumps and then finally applied a green antiseptic fluid. The casualty rolled his head and grimaced. He stared at his elevated, handless arms, blinked, and looked back as if to confirm what he was seeing, while Panasevich explained the accident to him. Theo looked down the road, half expecting an ambulance.

"This can't be a good omen," Panasevich turned away and whispered.

"I don't believe much in omens," Theo lied.

The medics loaded the division's first casualty onto a supply cart, instructing him to keep his arms elevated to prevent more blood loss and eventual shock. The soldier studied his bandages as if trying to solve a riddle. "Mój rączki, mój słodki rączki" (My hands, my sweet, sweet hands), he repeatedly murmured, holding up his stumps. "How will I support my family now without you?"

How, indeed, Theo grimaced. *The first waking thoughts of a Polish peasant: the welfare of his family!* He remembered his own instinctive reaction to Steffie blaming herself for Romko's death—to protect her somehow. "You know, Nature has a way of healing," he remembered telling her, as the waves from the oars began lapping onto the shore. She'd looked at him askance, so he explained. "Something we studied in physics; science and art both see different sides of the same beauty." He had felt her eyes on him, as if encouraging him, her blossoming knight in shining armor. "And do you know the most beautiful waves of all—the most healing—music! Music—nothing more than coherent soundwaves! Did you know that?"

She had sighed deeply, so he braved on with his increasingly clumsy monolog. "I found so much healing in Brahms and in Tchaikovsky." He'd concluded, "I really don't know if I could have managed, or gotten this far in life without my music, without its healing."

"I'm not surprised you'd say that, Theo," she had quickly rejoined, as if rescuing him from his own thin ice, and added that she played, too.

He turned to fully face her, knowing Steffie only from afar as a quick wit, and the life of the party, but a musician, too! "Which instrument?" he'd asked.

"Oh, the violin," she had answered emphatically. "In fact, I can't imagine life without it."

"Move out!" The division set off in the opposite direction, toward the rising sun, until they reached the familiar creek, and went off road, the carts skidding along the uneven slope, onto the wide, pebbly creek bed, past tree roots sticking out from the banks like palsied arms. Theo looked down the little valley, inclined on both sides, and sensed stillness, a sickly stillness, like in the field where he'd once seen a decaying dog beset by blue flies. He would have sent some scouts to reconnoiter before plunging the division into this short cut.

After about a kilometer, the wheels began sinking into soft sand, with the soldiers besetting the carts, pushing and pulling as if giving in to panic. The horses stumbled in the loose soil, and began rebelling against the lashes, their massive chests spotting with the white froth of thirst, the litter carrying the amputee sliding off the cart. Finally, a stallion collapsed and looked back like a wolf caught in a trap. Theo examined the horse's front leg and found it was bent at an unnatural angle. "Don't whip him!" he yelled. "Leg's broken."

Panasevich ran over and nodded toward the forward columns meandering around the creek's bend. "Just look!" he grumbled. "No flank security, no forward scouts—just this hurry to attack some invisible enemy," he said.

"Or to escape one," Theo countered.

Panasevich turned to the beast that was struggling to rise. "So what do we do?" he asked. "Cut him loose?"

Theo sighed. "Shoot him," he said.

"I've never shot a horse," Panasevich protested.

"What's holding us up?" the captain demanded, striding to the tilted supply cart. "Can't either of you shoot a damned horse?" He pointed his Radom officer's pistol at the horse's head. At that instant, the captain's head exploded, brain and bits of skull spurting across Theo's face. Another impact jerked Panasevich halfway around by his left shoulder. The captain dropped to his knees. Sand craters kicked up around them, bullets thudding against flesh. Panasevich staggered off toward his men, who began dropping like fruit from a shaken tree. Multiple flashes lit up the hillcrests, and Theo understood—they were caught in the kill zone of a classical ambush. A line of firing units blocked a retreat; a minefield blocked the way forward.

The impulse to protect his men detonated in his brain, as two trains collided in his mind, immobilizing his will. He knew what to do—if some part of him would just cut through the paralysis of that hideous eternity before his body awoke. "Mount the Brownings!" the scream finally broke out of his lungs. Of course! They had to counterattack head-to-head with the Germans along the creek—their only chance to survive the ambush. Three of his men ran toward the cart, through the whistling lead, and dropped. He saw the raw recruits instinctively herding together rather than spreading apart. The men he'd vowed to return were dropping their weapons, raising their hands, and getting cut down, body parts and horseflesh spurting through the air like a summer hailstorm. The bespectacled private, his jaw gone, wandered past Theo. Then the mortars began dropping.

All at once, the world fell silent. He saw the remaining men plodding on through the slow, protracted crimson shower toward the minefield. He became an actor in a silent movie. They reached the minefield. A severed leg careened slowly through the air, reminding him oddly of his only semester at medical school.

He knew he was living his last moments, his boots silently splashing up cascades of red creek water, while he stupidly recalled that these spilled fluids comprised seventy percent of the human body. So, this mix of detachment and euphoria was what it was like to die! On he staggered through the bloody mist, a ghost slowly traversing the bottom of a lake. But ahead in the forest, just ahead—could it be? Would he really get out of range? He reached the trees, knelt, and dropped his stained hands into the creek. Was he alive? He heard his name. Panasevich's voice!

All at once, the screams, neighs, grenades, and machine guns assaulted his ears like wolves bolting out of cages.

He turned to his left and to his right. How many had walked out? Just these forty or fifty—out of five hundred? He fell into the creek up to his ears, and rolled over, trying to catch his breath, and looked at the sky as he tasted the inferno in his throat. His tongue had swollen, dried out. His fingers found the canteen on his belt and unscrewed it.

A platoon of German soldiers stood at the edge of the clearing, pointing their guns at the survivors.

"Hände hoch!"

Theo recognized the command to surrender.

 A WEEK INTO THE INVASION, GERMAN EN-circlements were netting thousands of Polish prisoners. But the surrendering Poles—their government a signatory to the Geneva Convention on the Treatment of POWs—seemed confident their uniforms would protect them, give them POW status. Twenty-five miles from where Theo's regiment had run into an ambush, another Polish regiment being cut to pieces also surrendered.

During the surrender negotiations, a Polish sniper had shot dead a German officer. The German commander, Colonel Walter Wessel, ordered three hundred POWs to assemble to await further orders. Wessel's men found two German-speaking Poles from the POW ranks to translate Wessel's commands. The directive was simple: The detachment was to be shot as out-of-uniform guerrillas—without Geneva Convention protection. The trench was nearly dug. The detachment of POWs had merely to finish it.

Retaliation against guerilla warfare had been standard military practice for Western armies for decades. European and American military manuals recommended shooting hostages to maintain order in the event of serious insurrections, but this was recommended in the context of hostages being *civilian*, not POWs, members of the military.

THEO ROSE FROM HIS KNEES, THREW HIS HANDS UP, and saw the division's remnants, blood and fragments covering everyone's coats like vomitus. He averted his eyes from a Pole pulling in his glistening intestines. *My God, how far had that poor devil walked like that?* Panasevich staggered into view, his right arm against his drenched coat sleeve. He smiled wearily and winked.

"Hände hoch!" the command repeated.

Panko dropped his good hand as if to undo his belt buckle. *Didn't he understand?!* Theo gasped. *Didn't the Poles?* A bullet whistled past, knocking Panko backwards. Theo stepped toward his writhing companion, but the sergeant ordered, "Sofort! Hier sammeln!" and pointed to a wide sandbank underneath the trees. The Poles stayed frozen in place.

"Form up there!" Theo yelled in Polish. "There! Along the stream!" Theo saw an automatic weapon pointing at him, as another command demanded his silence. "Please!" Theo called out in German, and looked away to control his nausea. "I'm just translating." The survivors stumbled into the clearing, trying to form into lines.

Soldiers in well-cut field-gray tunics—as elegant as any uniforms Theo had seen—separated the Polish enlisted men from the officers. *The little collar zigzags make it easy enough to identify us,* Theo thought. He didn't recognize anyone among the survivors—no, wait, could that pale shadow be Jacek from his officer candidate class? Had their class sidekick somehow survived? He remembered listening to his homespun forays into ancient religion and astrology half into the night.

Leica cameras clicked open. Several Germans took turns posing with a captive officer, who had a pronounced, dark crotch stain. Theo didn't recognize the poor wretch, who'd hung his head. A freckled soldier clicked a pocketknife open, joked with his friends, and cut away three Polish eagle buttons from Theo's woolen tunic. He wiped the buttons off and dropped them into his side pocket. Theo wondered if this generation of young Germans had grown up differently from the one who had once quartered in his father's house.

The captives marched out under guard onto a paved road, Theo's popped blisters rubbing against his wet boots. A machine gun chattered from behind him, probably from the clearing, their point of surrender. Who would inform Panko's parents? Theo agonized.

German soldiers were stacking discarded Polish rifles and helmets along the road into long rectangular piles, along with tungsten-tipped anti-tank rounds and a few medium howitzers. They reached a railroad siding, and passed a trio of field-grade officers drinking from white metal mugs around a table that held telephone-switching gear. Strains of victorious martial music flowed from the tall command tents behind them.

They marched to an improvised barbed-wire enclosure with hundreds of milling Polish officers. As the column approached the gate, angry words caught Theo's ears: "What's holding up our Allies?" and "We were betrayed!" But the conversation ceased at the spectacle they were making as they walked through the gate, covered in muck, as if they wore the uniforms of an alien army.

Theo avoided their extended hands. He'd never really developed the knack of finding comfort by sharing his misery. He parried their questions and found a spot on the yellow grass where he tried to control the tremors beginning to shake his body. He heard a Polish officer behind him speak endearingly about his expectant wife, Danuta. Theo sat and twisted his marriage ring until the skin chafed.

He remembered once reading Steffie his secret poetry – the dark stuff he'd written once as an outcast, a semi-orphan. He had wanted to unburden himself and took a risk. Would this woman with her uncommon intuition give him insight, loosen some straps confining his soul? He knew that total strangers revealed their innermost turmoil to her – even rugged men like Slota confessed their secrets. What was it about her that drew people out?

Steffie could observe and grasp people's essence at a glance. Those black eyes took in everything. She could imitate the speech, posture, and even beliefs of anyone she met – and give impersonations that made friends gasp or howl with delight. Maybe that's what he'd sensed in her – a mirror, instant recognition.

He remembered when Steffie began coming to *Prosvita* meetings. Her sultry looks and drop-dead imitations of Europe's political figures had totally captivated him, not to mention the rest of the bachelors as well! Awkward at repartee, he'd felt left out in the social banter among his colleagues, and thought he was in danger of losing her, until the evening the two of them had volunteered to stay late to print copies of a grammar book for Ukrainian villagers, again, in defiance of Polish authorities. Alone together, he could do no better than stammer non-sequiturs, changing topics every sentence, until she'd burst out laughing. He saw her grinning, seemingly taking him in all at once. "So, ask me," he remembered her saying. *Ask her what?* Theo had thought, struggling with a response. "Do you want me to be your wife?"

He had felt a window burst open in his heart, letting in the sunshine, along with the purest crystalline snow and the warmest rain.

And now, her parting words kept resurfacing, despite himself: "Theo, you know I love you"; and "Theo, why are you doing this to us?"

He was despairing of finding any clarity, when the groan of heavy engines distracted him. The POWs were standing at the fence staring through the wire at a military policeman directing a column of Mercedes cargo trucks, their tightened, half-drawn canvases revealing their dark interiors as they parked side by side. Theo recognized the sergeant from his capture pointing him out to a lieutenant.

"Du—komm her!" the sergeant yelled, and motioned Theo toward the gate.

Theo made his way through the Poles, who eyed him suspiciously. True, why would this officer pick him out of the horde of POWs? Theo saw the intelligent face of a German aristocrat, and saluted. The officer brushed his swagger stick against the empty buttonholes of Theo's soiled tunic. "Officers deserve their respect," he murmured to the sergeant, "regardless of the army they fight for." He turned to Theo. "The sergeant says you know German."

Theo smoothed his caked trousers. "Ja, Herr Leutnant." He tried to keep his voice from cracking. "My, my father taught me."

"Ah! Another generation entirely," the officer observed. "Well, we'll see how well he did. Come!"

As they approached the idling trucks, Theo's soul shrank, realizing the Germans wanted him to interpret; maybe at interrogation sessions. Well, he'd have to refuse. He'd cite the Geneva Convention. Nor would he admit to being Ukrainian. No, he'd insist that he remain with his comrades. He heard the heavy steps of the armed guards behind him as they passed the quartet of command tents. As the forest loomed ahead, the silly thought occurred that maybe they'd just keep marching on, right into a new zone, into a new era. But he knew the officer would eventually stop and make an impossible demand.

At a grassy knoll, the officer pulled out his Luger and told the sergeant he would handle the prisoner from there. Was this going to be an execution? What had he done? The officer told Theo to walk toward the edge of the forest, and holstered his sleek black pistol. They halted, and the officer measured him with the eye of a tailor, Theo thought, or maybe that of an undertaker. "So what kind of lessons did your father give you?" the officer asked.

"My father?" Theo repeated. "We read the poets together."

The officer tilted his head. "Poets? German poets?"

Theo paused and nodded. "Yes, Rilke. My father liked Rilke."

"What did he like about Rilke?"

"He called him a gentle companion, a companion for solitude."

The officer nodded. "I like Rilke, too," he said, "Go on."

"Well, he often quoted that line about spring," Theo went on. "'Spring is a prodigy, a child that only speaks in rhymes.'" Theo felt a release of tension as a smile broke over the officer's face; like one of those moments when grace had whispered the right thing to say, and he'd said it. The officer pulled a cigarette packet out of his pocket, and Theo added, "In fact, Rilke reminds me of Franko, one of our own poets."

"Franko? Never heard of him. A Polish poet?" The officer asked.

Theo refused the cigarette. "No, not, not Polish," Theo stammered.

"No?" The officer struck a match. "I thought you were—"

"We read others, too!" Theo interjected. "I personally prefer Heine, his love poems—"

"Heine?" the officer interrupted, and inhaled. "He wrote in German, but he was no Aryan."

No Aryan! Theo thought. *Wasn't that some tribe that roamed ancient Persia, or somewhere? Shaggy-haired men with bare-breasted cohorts in whalebone necklaces who chanted around campfires?* What did he mean, Heine wasn't Aryan?

The officer peered into his captive's face. "But Aryan blood must flow in your veins," he insisted, and tapped his cigarette against the case.

The officer might as well have asked if Theo had been hatched from an egg. Were these Aryans somehow connected to the new Germany, Theo wondered? A truck horn broke his concentration. "Well, yes, it's possible," he said.

Another truck convoy pulled up along the railroad siding. As the engines coughed to a halt, squads of German soldiers raised and pointed their rifles.

"Dienst ist Dienst," the officer said, and told the sergeant to take Theo back.

Inside the barbed wire, Theo had stepped onto the wobbly foot bridge crossing the creek, when two POWs came up and blocked his path. *Well, the Poles are nothing,* Theo thought, *if not excitable.*

A young officer with the sultry looks of a silent screen film star demanded, "Well, why are they keeping us like this? In the open, like cattle?"

His older companion—overcoat draped around his shoulders in the French way—rebuked him. "No, they must need us for something, something big. No one would just waste officers." His eyes pleaded with Theo for corroboration.

"We discussed literature," Theo said, "nothing more," and took a step past them, but saw more POWs sauntering down toward them.

"German literature?" the sultry-faced officer asked with a hint of sarcasm. He looked at his comrades, and added, "Exactly whose side are you on? I can't really place your accent."

"And I can't place yours," Theo shot back. He stopped and turned. "I wouldn't worry. Germany signed the Geneva Convention," he added. "Germans keep their word."

"So what exactly is their word?"

"Gentlemen," someone in the crowd tried to break in, as Theo walked away.

Theo spent a sleepless hour trying to identify a few of the better-known constellations, but instead of finding relief, the vastness of the night sky oppressed him almost as much as his thirst. He wandered through the cluster of makeshift bonfires stooping to look for familiar faces. He found Jacek, who greeted him, "Theo – an officer born like us under an auspicious star!" Jacek had attracted another rapt audience reclining together on the cool grass.

"Auspicious?" a lieutenant in a still-immaculate uniform asked, "What about the rumor they'll transfer the lot of us to a prison camp tomorrow?"

"Rumors," Jacek said in mock seriousness. "Man lives not by rumors alone."

"I suppose you'll next tell us our fates are written in the stars," the officer said.

Jacek looked beyond the treetops and said, "We're fools to ignore astrology. Ten years ago, when we were all still boys, an Indian astrologer announced that August and September of this year would shatter the peace of Europe. And here we are."

"Well, alright, he got lucky. Anyone can be lucky once," the officer said. "I myself believe in science, logic, reason, not in this, this ... But, okay ...," he added, "what else did he predict?"

Jacek turned over on his back. "Our destiny," he said and pointed, "is already mapped out. There's Andromeda, that bright cluster there – the Charmed Lady they call her – but to me, our own sweet Mother Poland. And now look just to the east – there's the Dragon ... the Dragon threatening our mother."

"Where exactly do you see a dragon?" Theo asked.

"Those five stars," Jacek said, "The dragon's eyes, wings ... the tip of the tail. And now look below Andromeda, just below – Pegasus, the Winged Horse, *le cheval ailé* – who else could he be but a French cavalier galloping to Mother Poland's rescue." He turned to the stylish officer and said, "If the future holds a prison camp for us, it won't last long."

"Why does the Dragon attack from the east?" Theo objected, "Germany attacked us from the west."

Jacek shrugged. "My grandmother once said that the stars can't lie."

As he drifted off amid the brisk night breezes and the crackling of the fire, Theo wondered if somewhere among those stars, a pair of eyes wasn't watching over him.

The next morning the groan of heavy engines awoke him. The rising sun brought a little warmth, but without alleviating his thirst; the stream had gone muddy. POWs were already crowded at the fence, staring through the barbed wire. A military policeman was directing an incoming column of trucks that turned and parked side-by-side – revealing more Polish officers through their tightened, half-drawn canvases. Theo sensed a pair of eyes on him and recognized the sergeant from his capture pointing him out to a lieutenant.

The German lieutenant called him out and clenched his teeth. "Herr Leutnant," he muttered, "you come from eastern Poland." He tapped another cigarette against his engraved case, first gently, then vigorously. "You must know the Russians. Tell me about them."

"You mean their writers, poets?" Theo began.

"You know I don't mean that," the lieutenant interjected, and turned suddenly to the shriek of a train whistle.

Theo knew a wrong answer might likely seal his fate. After all, the Germans and Russians had just become allies. "I only know the Russians from friends' accounts," he said slowly. "For sure, they admire strength, victory at any price. Ruthless!" He saw the puffs of coal-fired clouds entering the station.

The lieutenant nodded and lit the cigarette. "Then you know what awaits you," he said, "if we turn you over to the Russians."

"But why on earth would you do that?" Theo asked.

A mighty train engine labored against its own inertia, grinding metal against metal. Wooden boxcars, one after another, rolled into the station, and astride the roofs; uniformed men, with hints of blue glinting from their caps, each one grasping an impossibly long rifle. All at once, the engine choked in a cloud of steam, and the men atop braced for a halt that came with an ear-splitting screech. Theo doubted that at this distance he could recognize any of the Polish officers already waiting in columns.

"Listen carefully," the lieutenant said, and dropped his cigarette and crushed it. "Right now, we're transferring you"—he paused— "all of you Polish officers to the Russians." Theo clearly read the contempt in his eyes.

"But why, Herr Leutnant?" Theo asked again.

"You haven't heard? The Red Army invaded Poland yesterday."

Theo realized the lieutenant had dodged his question; if the Poles were POWs of the Germans, why transfer them to the Russians?

"Walk straight into the forest," the lieutenant said. "Don't look back. I'd better not see you when I turn around."

What did that mean? He'd better escape? Or he'd better not?

Who didn't know this trick, talking a prisoner into escaping and shooting him? He glanced at the unstrapped holster holding the Luger, and grasped the choice: probable death if the Russians took him, possible death if he walked away.

He took two, four, eight steps, half expecting to hear the click of the round entering the chamber. Would the hot lead hurt or kill him instantly? The forest finally swallowed him, and his head swam. He walked until he felt the sun on his skin, until he felt his legs again, until he heard insects buzzing and branches snapping under his boots, until he reached a clearing with a view of the open fields, the same fields that men were fighting and killing for. He turned and saw a stand of trees guarding his escape like a squadron of mottled angels.

SIMPLE PRAGMATISM, AND NOTHING ELSE, had driven two sworn enemies, Hitler and Stalin, to drop their antagonism and to cooperate temporarily. Their Non-Aggression Pact was addressing deep anxieties that both dictators faced. Hitler feared that any naval blockades Britain was planning against Germany would choke off the import of iron ore and rubber, without which, his military machine would march to a halt. Just as crucially, Hitler had promised that his nation would never go hungry again; starvation had stalked German streets during World War I, and the German diet depended heavily on grain imports. Stalin agreed to satisfy these needs with generous shipments of both metal and wheat, commodities in jeopardy as another world war had threatened.

What did Stalin get in return from an enemy that—in Hitler's widely read *Mein Kampf*— had vowed to do no less than destroy the Soviet Union? Hitler recognized that Stalin was facing his own fears of survival. How was Russia going to stop Japan's bold military advance into her eastern territories? Japan, Russia's hereditary enemy, now fielded a modern, mechanized army. Hitler promised to transfer Germany's finest warplanes and tanks to Russia, and even pledged to help Stalin assemble a first-rate navy.

Beyond this mutually beneficial deal, the two conspirators had also decided to help themselves to more land. Hitler and Stalin agreed to divide the territory historically caught between Russia and Germany, land that Germans often referred to as *Zwischeneuropa*, or "residual Europe."

Stalin began by claiming lands that the Versailles, Treaty had taken earlier from Czarist Russia—the Baltic countries, some ethnic Ukrainian territory, and part of Finland—and the list was to grow.

Hitler, for his part, began by claiming the original slices of Germany that Versailles had ceded to Poland. Both sides also agreed to carve up the remainder of Poland between them. Few living in eastern Europe knew where the new demarcation line would fall—a line that would plunge them into either the unbending grasp of Hitler's Reich or Stalin's Communist State.

BEREZA KARTUSKA, THE MAIN POLISH DETENTION
camp for political prisoners, stood square in the path of the invading Red Army—and about 150 miles north of Theo's ambush site.
Ukrainians referred to Bereza as a "concentration camp," and for good
reason. For its design, the Poles had borrowed the prison specifica-
tions from an unlikely source—from the notorious Gulag, the Soviet
penal system. Bereza Kartuska exactly duplicated the Gulag's approach
to confining and handling political prisoners: double electrified wires,
cadres of amateur but preferably psychopathic guards, a regime of un-
ending harassment, such as ceaselessly interrupting prisoners' sleep,
spiking their food with insects and sawdust, limiting prisoners' time to
relieve themselves to daily forty-second periods, and finally, non-stop
labor designed to break even the strongest prisoner's health.

As war threatened, the prison's population swelled to over ten
thousand, most of them Ukrainian nationalists, Polish Communists,
and even rebellious Polish journalists, such as the author of an article titled, "Five Minutes to Twelve," published in the Polish magazine
Bunt Młodych.

"We don't know how to deal with our minorities," the article read.
"Our policies have led Ukrainians to desperation, and we refuse to recognize how we ourselves drove them there.... And the result? The OUN
is now stronger than all the other Ukrainian political parties combined."

One such OUN operative at the prison, Theo's brother-in-law
Viktor, heard the steps of approaching guards one scorching summer
morning. After three weeks on half rations—and less oxygen—in the
small, white airtight structure equipped for solitary confinement, the
prisoner Viktor Sabat should, as a rule, be easy to handle. How had the
twenty-five-year-old newlywed ended up here?

In his boyhood, the orphaned Viktor Sabat had gone to live with
his uncle. Viktor's father had died—some would say a hero's death—in
the ill-fated Ukrainian Galician Army. The band of suicidally patriotic

men marched out against absurd odds—their idealistic and impractical campaign typical in Ukrainian history. The group enjoyed initial successes, until at last, low on ammunition and reduced to maneuvering and zigzagging—and finally encircled and trapped—they succumbed in scores to the Typhus epidemic and perished into legend and into history. His uncle could see that Viktor had revered his father's memory, sometimes humming the stirring marching songs to himself from that army's famous but quixotic campaign to rid Ukrainian lands of no less than four enemy armies.

Viktor's uncle had found solace from his brother's death in the age-old distraction of gambling; weeks at a time behind a poker table, a bottle always at his side, refusing to give one goddamn again about any independence movement that would run aground anyway, and lead to family tragedy. Viktor had felt torn between his uncle, a worldly rogue and glib talker, and the memory of his own idealistic father. His uncle had noticed a knack for deal-making in his nephew, and encouraged the boy to forget all this nationalistic nonsense. A clever man could make a fortune in the black market outwitting Polish import restrictions.

One fine day, Viktor had realized that both paths—his father's and his uncle's—involved gambling against the odds, but that his father had somehow chosen the higher, nobler stakes. He broke with his uncle and joined the OUN, where his bravery had quickly outpaced his knowledge of how to outwit the police. After a series of arrests, a Polish judge designated him a serious security threat.

And now, peering into the abrupt sunlight, the five-foot-five-inch Viktor staggered out to screams of "Marsh, sukinsynu!" Three months in prison had emphasized every bone in his short frame and handsome, Mongolian-looking face. And now with hunger and thirst clouding his mind, Viktor bent down for his prison wooden clogs and spotted a crushed cigarette butt, and deftly scooped up the prison's most valuable

ESCAPES

exchange commodity. If the guards had noticed the maneuver, he knew their clubs would quickly turn him into a writhing dog.

Viktor found his sixty cellmates strangely not at work, but crammed together in ankle-high water awaiting some order, some news. Viktor passed the butt to Roman, the inmate who'd first taken him under his wing, instructing him night after night in the secrets of the OUN underground, and tricks to outwit the police. Eyes flashing in gratitude, Roman regretted he couldn't offer a scrap of bread or a shred of pork-belly skin in return. Then the order came to slog out again; double time in their clumsy clogs.

Clomping past the reeking kitchen, Viktor noticed the guards in their three pointed caps getting distracted pummeling an older prisoner senseless, who'd stumbled and fallen in the crowded hallway. Viktor bolted from the line and pushed over a cooking pot nearly his own height, knelt, and peered in. As the guards ran in, Viktor curled in, scraping out burnt buckwheat that caked the bottom. The guards clanged on the side until his head emerged, blackened and greasy, defiantly chewing. They held him up and looked back at the sergeant, who motioned to let him have it. His wire-hard body stiffening against the clubs, Viktor dodged the first few swings.

"Why give them the satisfaction?" Roman whispered as they emerged into the sunlight. "Dignity, Viktor, your best revenge!"

Outside, the prison complex had the look of a converted monastery: austere but tidy. The prisoners came to a halt in front of a half-dug trench that bore the look of workers repairing a sewer line. The air smelled waterlogged. Viktor glanced down the line and then past the buildings to the reddening trees. The Pripet marshes began somewhere beyond the barbed wire.

"How would anyone escaping know how to navigate past the wires?" Roman whispered, "A hundred miles of marsh, even quicksand in places."

"What's been going on since I left for solitary?" Viktor whispered. "I overheard snatches of Radio Warsaw."

Roman looked askance at Viktor and nodded. "Shhh! The Polish Army abandoned Warsaw. The guards locked us up and debated what the hell to do." He looked around and added, "Yesterday, they executed two captured German soldiers brought in for interrogation."

"If they're distracted, this could be our chance to escape," Viktor said.

They turned their attention to the camp commander, a bulky man with thick spectacles perched on a generous nose—the inmates called him "The Hippo"—covering the parade grounds as quickly as his short legs permitted. He nodded to the guards, who ordered the prisoners to jump in and pick up the shovels.

Viktor's shovel slammed into the trench and emitted a clean sound, the metallic ping of striking rock. He moved a leg forward to swivel the weight of the earth, and tossed out a shovelful. Brown Belorussian earth flew up all along the ditch. The prisoners, as condemned men had done for centuries, dug their own mass grave. Viktor, still bleeding from his ears, raised his shovel like an ax as a guard passed but dropped the tip at the drone of an engine—a wide-winged aircraft coasting in the evening sky.

"Skurwysyn! Not one of ours!" the sergeant yelled.

 AFTER THE MIRACLE OF THE VISTULA, where Polish forces, with Ukrainian help, had defeated a much larger Red Army in 1920, the warring sides had sat down to the negotiating table. The victorious Poles, promising to represent Ukrainian interests, negotiated a deal directly with Moscow. The agreement left their Ukrainian allies with exactly nothing. The Poles took western Ukraine; the Russians retained the rest of the country. The Western Allies formally

recognized the new borders—a particularly bitter experience for western Ukrainians, who had earlier declared a republic out of the ruins of World War I, and had fought bravely, doggedly against multiple foes to try to keep their independence. Surviving Ukrainian generals, feeling betrayed, decided they'd been on a fool's errand with their aboveboard approach to independence—honor in the officer corps, conventional armed forces, binding treaties and alliances—and all of that had left them empty-handed. They resolved now to take the low road—to destabilize western Ukraine's new Polish government, which they considered illegitimate—through planned hit-and-run tactics and even political assassinations, even at the highest levels. Hell hath no fury, they might have conceded, like an ally scorned.

Most Ukrainians, however, acknowledged that the game had fundamentally changed—at least for now—but decided instead to work within the new Polish system. And so much work needed to be done to rebuild after the war—work to spread literacy, to preserve Ukrainian culture, and to develop the economically backward Ukrainian countryside—initiatives that could bloom only in peacetime. They organized themselves into a broad political party that called itself the Ukrainian National Democratic Alliance, the UNDO, and, embracing western European ideals, opened multiple economic and cultural fronts in an astonishing display of volunteerism.

Like most of the western Ukrainian intelligentsia, the Wozniaks enthusiastically embraced the UNDO, and worked to lift their countrymen up, organizing farming cooperatives, credit unions, and literacy programs, all of it legally to avoid provoking Polish reprisals.

The farming cooperative movement, in particular, represented a triumph of intelligent Ukrainian persistence in the face of Polish antagonism to any independent Ukrainian economic development. Ukrainians in the UNDO saw the cooperative movement not only as a tool for economic progress, but also as a school for self-government—right in the midst of the Polish occupiers. Ukrainian middlemen cut out the Poles by simply buying Ukrainian farming and dairy products, processing them, and reselling them throughout the country. The Ukrainian cooperative movement even successfully penetrated western European markets, permitting farmers to escape poverty, while employing tens of thousands of otherwise unemployed Ukrainian workers. The UNDO recognized Theo's brother-in-law, Slavko Wozniak, a surprisingly quiet and diplomatic man, as one of the most astute directors of the main dairy cooperative, MasloSoyuz—no simple task in western Ukraine's multiethnic cauldron. And hopefully, one fine day, after western Ukrainians had built up their political skills and economic power, the UNDO would negotiate independence itself for western Ukraine! Such was the hope.

Nevertheless, the fringe group of former Ukrainian military officers and its hard-core resisters rejected the UNDO's approach, and in fact declared cooperation of any kind with the Poles as treason! This radical group declared itself the Organization of Ukrainian Nationalists, the OUN. The Nationalists, to which Viktor swore allegiance, not only reemphasized violence, but expanded its policy of assassinations to include any prominent Ukrainians cooperating with the Poles. Adherents of both rival approaches—the UNDO and the OUN—sometimes found themselves living under one roof.

ON THE THIRD DAY OF HIS UNEASY FREEDOM, THEO located the Vistula River, but not before seeing horrifying Polish atrocities against Germans – German villages burned down; their families herded together and beaten to death. In a way, he understood this Polish outrage at the German invasion, this scream for revenge. Didn't Ukrainians feel the same way about the Poles?

The first two bridges he found looked as if some drunken giants had smashed the roadways and kicked the trusses into the fast-flowing river. He found the only undamaged bridge further upstream, but under heavy guard, with campfires flickering on the banks across the river. Refugees? Military units? Beyond them, eastern Galicia, where his native Ukrainians well outnumbered the Poles. He chose a spot further upriver and waited for dawn.

How would he plan his next move? Across the river, he could head east, back to his native Hadynkivtsi, where he knew he belonged in the middle of this manmade calamity, where he could at least protect his two sisters and his maimed father; but he could also head south, back to Kalush to face his disillusionment, to resolve his marriage—another mission altogether. Whatever he did, who would really know in the middle of this chaos? They'd assume that the war had just taken him, like it had taken so many others, but . . . but was that how a man of character behaved?

One in ten survived the ambush, and he knew that one in a thousand walked out of the POW camp. What was fate saving him for?

After the last nightingale's song, light began breaking on a gray world seemingly drained of all reason. A cloud of morning mist rose up across the fast-moving stream—the perfect cover for a swimmer. The dark silhouette of a fish broke the surface, and then another. He waded into the cold water – the mud silky against his feet – and swam. Midway across, an iron-hard pair of jaws clamped onto his calf and pierced the muscle. He kicked to free himself, and felt another pair of punctures—no, not fish—cramps, cramps! Trying to straighten his contorted legs, he felt his right arm cramp, too, and then the other. Was this then the end? He cried out to the God that his mother once prayed to. He subdued his panic and remembered somehow to float. Fatigue, he realized. Just fatigue!

After wading ashore, he heard the crackle of a rifle and took cover – just some poorly aimed pot shots. He hid, discarded his soaked Polish army tunic, and appropriated a shirt from a clothesline. He heard soon enough that the German military had commandeered the trains, and a rumor that the Red Army was advancing this way from the northeast. He realized he was moving through a momentary lull between two approaching storms, a political vacuum where all law and order had broken down, and so atrocities were flourishing just as savagely on this side of the river, too—this time, Ukrainians chasing down and murdering Polish aristocracy, usually in ghastly and inventive ways, with farm tools.

He found himself in a column of refugees heading east, Polish farmers, in their leather hats, and their long-skirted women balancing suitcases from one shoulder to another, their wide-eyed children hauling shoulder sacks. "Why aren't you with your unit defending us?" Theo heard a woman's voice behind him.

But then another woman's voice instantly responded, "He'll fight again. *Jeszcze Polska nie zginęla*! [Poland is not yet lost!]" Passenger cars beeped their way through the crowds, all trying to outrun the German invaders, until the human bedlam reached a twisted railroad bridge, still partially intact, spanning a gorge, where an unexpected line of refugees scrambled at them from the opposite direction, yelling, "Go back! Go back! Russians! Russians heading this way!"

The refugee column split along both sides of the river. Theo suddenly remembered Viktor. If the Reds had penetrated this far, they would have already overrun the Bereza prison, where his brother-in-law, together with thousands of other nationalists, all cooped up neatly like sheep in pens, awaited the anti-Ukrainian invaders.

THE 21ˢᵀ CENTURY

A REALITY CHECK

H istory always came alive for me in Holy Trinity Church, a rough-hewn structure of bold angles and soaring spaces, in fact, a board-by-board replica from Ukraine's Cossack past. After breathing in the incense and feeling the Byzantine chants resonate in my chest, I left Mass in an elevated mood, and gunned my Plymouth Voyager south on Georgia Avenue. Turning into a labyrinth of suburban streets, I finally spotted the twin sprawling bushes that flanked my sister's driveway in Silver Spring, Maryland.

I found my father's bed empty. Books in four languages lined the walls on either side of his bed. He was still in love with books – links, really, to his friends, his vanished community. Many bore titles like *An Era of Terrors, Surviving a Death Camp, Life in the Time of Yezhov's Secret Police,* and *Banished to Kazakhstan* – most written in Ukrainian: survivors' memoirs of the Socialisms that Stalin and Hitler had thrust on Europe. Printed in the 1940s on inexpensive stock, the books were yellowing – the edges of the outer pages crumpling like cigarette ashes

– the experiences of an entire generation disintegrating, passing unknown into history.

I saw three books he must have neatly stacked on the side table – probably for me – a trilogy of some kind in rough cloth binding.

I opened the first volume to the title page, *Vom Tsarenadler zur Roten Fahne*. A photo of P. N. Krasnow, an aristocratically dressed, solemn man in his fifties, stared out from the opposite page.

I heard my father's voice, his laughter in the hallway. He stood unassisted, attending a guest, Dr. Kalynovich, an elderly friend from the war years. My father turned toward me with that gesture so familiar from the photo albums of his bachelor years—his arms akimbo, head tilted back, his face radiant—the last time I'd see him as an oak, sturdy and solid in the orchard, while the winds quietly gathered strength. I noticed he trembled slightly.

The Sunday before, he'd made light of my writing project, telling me it wouldn't amount to much. And now, as he told Dr. Kalynovich I was trying to write a book on the war, he chuckled, the way a father chuckles as his toddler swings a plastic hammer. The guest's eyes smiled in sympathy.

Back in the makeshift bedroom, Tato handed me the topmost book. "Here, if you want to consult a serious work on war," he said, and lowered himself, joint by joint, onto the bed, like fragile cargo settling slowly on the dock. He looked at me testily. "You do read some German, don't you?"

"*From the Czar's Eagle to the Red Banner*," I translated, relieved that I'd recognized each word in the title without a dictionary.

"A novel about the Russian Revolution, a German translation from the original Russian. Read it," he said, his eyes flashing as if delivering a checkmate, "and you'll find all you need to know." I knew the book had once transfixed him, and especially one grisly scene between a father and son caught on opposite sides of the revolution.

"You mean, all I need to know about how to write?" I asked, afraid that he was going to cancel our interview today, or worse.

"About war as it really is," he said. "How it unmasks human nature, what people are willing to do to others when law breaks down. How we don't really know ourselves – until we're tested." He closed his eyes and added, almost too quietly to hear, "How it exposed my own weaknesses."

Weaknesses, I thought and dropped the crusty book back on his night table. I knew of dozens of refugees he had resettled after the war, and I knew of the relatives he had helped to survive the era. "Or maybe your own heroism?" I suggested to provoke a deeper response.

"Heroism?" He shook his head. "No, not heroism – survival! Think of how you would you feel if you saw, say, Chinese or Islamic tanks moving down the Beltway? Heroic? I was wearing a Polish uniform, not a Ukrainian uniform, while we were left without an army of our own to defend ourselves."

I felt history coming alive again and picked up my notebook to take notes.

SEPTEMBER 17, 1939

THE CHANGE OF POWER

The end of the summer 1939 changed eastern Europe's borders at the cost of hundreds of thousands of casualties. Word had yet not reached Kalush on the fate of her sons.

The store shelves quickly emptied, but life had to go on. Maria Wozniak sent her two daughters into the family garden with instructions to watch out for looters. Zosia chopped her shovel into the black soil and turned over the moist earth. "Disgusting!" she said. "I just cut an earthworm in two. Look! Both halves are moving."

Steffie knelt at her sister's feet. "The little thing is suffering," she said.

Zosia nodded. "And now both sides are suffering."

"How long since we've seen them, Zosia? Do you think either one is still alive?"

"Don't even think about that. That's a sure way to go crazy!" Zosia pushed the blade back down. "Hey, I just hit something!" Birds perching on the barren branches cocked their heads as if to see what the shovel unearthed.

Steffie pulled out a large, clumpy potato and brushed away the moist dirt. "Do you think he'll return to me?" She swung her arm, and the pail clanged.

"Why did you mislead him? Why take such a risk?" Zosia pushed the shovel down again. "Didn't you think he'd find out eventually?"

"What woman doesn't stretch the truth to get her man? I thought he'd get used to me, and our love would grow."

"I see. He'd become too enamored with all your good points."

"Don't be sarcastic."

"Maybe it's God's will, Steffie." Zosia looked out at the gray plateau of clouds catching fire. "You know Mama didn't think he was right for you."

"But Tato did."

"If he returns, ask him to forgive you."

"He'd never forgive me."

"You mean you'd never ask."

They heard their mother limp out onto the porch. "Any news?" Steffie called out.

"We can't catch Radio Warsaw right now," Maria Wozniak said, "but I'm not expecting anything but the usual Polish bravado." She turned to a figure standing behind the fence. "Mrs. Panasevich! So festively dressed today!"

Zosia lifted her pail. The neighbor leaned in, her red coral necklace dangling. "No, keep them," she whispered and patted Zosia's hand. "You've got a big family. You'll need more now – now that Warsaw fell!" She straightened out – her eyes oddly unfocused. "Our boys are coming home!" she proclaimed.

"Warsaw fell, you said?" Zosia asked. "And what about the prisons?"

Mrs. Panasevich looked out from the hilltop at the long, green park below. "They should be returning today my Roman and your

Theo. They served together, you know." "Pani Maria, I came to ask for a little confectionary sugar; for *pampushky*, my Romko's favorite."

"Time for *pampushky* already?" Maria Wozniak asked, "But how did you hear?" She turned to see Steffie running for the shed. "Wait! What if it's a rumor?" she yelled as Zosia strode across the yard.

Maria Wozniak limped toward the gate and held out her cane like a crossbeam as Steffie approached. "It's not safe now! The curfew!" She lowered her voice, "Steffie, please! She's just a confused old widow. She doesn't know." Mother and daughter looked each other in the eye. "Steffie, if he comes back at all, let him come here instead! Don't risk yourself for him! You don't even know –!"

"Mama, you're wrong! I know him," Steffie said, "– better even than he knows himself!" She yanked, trying to maneuver the handlebars out of her sister's grip.

BY THE END OF SEPTEMBER, POLAND ceased to exist. The two invaders imprisoned hundreds of thousands of Polish soldiers, the remnants scattering across the border. The Polish government fled to France. Theo, the Wozniaks, and Galicians of all ethnicities awaited their new masters. But were the Germans and Russians splitting up Poland as allies—or as competing sharks? The Germans had advanced as far as L'viv, but then suddenly withdrew. Eyewitnesses reported a pitched battle between Germans and Russians north of Kalush. But others reported a joint German-Russian military parade in the town of Brest-Litovsk.

THE APARTMENT BUILDING LOOKED VAGUELY FAMIL-
iar, as if staring at a dollhouse. The same two clay rabbits he had
sculpted still framed the bay window, welcoming, playful, but their
very innocence crumpled his soul. In the hallway, an older man in an
Edwardian moustache thudded toward him with a cane, his steps echoing through the corridor, his mutt whining at the street noises and
pausing to sniff him. The man stopped to glare. "Don't you recognize
me?" Theo asked.

"Deserter?" the man asked in Polish, shaking his head. "Safer at
home, isn't it?"

Deserter, Theo silently repeated to himself. Maybe he was. He certainly seemed to lack the nerve to face Steffie's family. They'd know
by now how he'd treated her. When the thumping turned the corner,
Theo reached to knock, remembered, and checked for the spare key
behind the ledge.

He found his oasis the way he had left it: with its clockwork or-
derliness. He ran a finger over the clock's curved, polished surface, and
reset it and wound it, the ticking filling the silence. The bookcases of
classical literature in three languages still stood at attention, awaiting
his next order. The corked bottles of photographic development solu-
tions stood patiently in the shadows of the lower shelf. He saw no sign
at all that Steffie had visited, and in the stillness, clicked on the shortwave radio and dialed to Warsaw.

Instead of Polish, a gravelly foreign voice came on. Russian?!
Strange, that for two so-called fraternal languages—Ukrainian and
Russian—he still couldn't decipher the message. What did *rasprostra-
nyeyiye* and *pereraspredeleniye* mean, those strange polysyllabic words?
Turning up the volume didn't help. Something in the tone of the
broadcast put him on alert. He listened until the Communist anthem
came on, the seductive hymn proclaiming international brotherhood.
Did a new era really await them? He had instead found their slogans

unsettling: "The personal life in Russia is dead"; and "All art must serve the proletariat." Really? All art? What about the music of Tchaikovsky, Rimsky-Korsakoff, and Stravinsky? Did their music not stir men's souls beyond what economic theories ever could?

He clicked off the radio and reached for his soulmate, unsnapped the case, and touched the bow to the still-taut string. Before he could cull out the first sound, Steffie gently pulled down his right arm.

"Theo, you've come back," she whispered, the evening light streaming in from the window, burnishing her hair. "I thought you might have found someone else."

NAZI IDEOLOGY DECLARED THE VOLK, the simplest of Germany's people, to be the nation's supreme asset. The Nazis exalted the village folk—for their work ethic, their practicality, their unpretentious art. Tilling the soil, raising animals, witnessing the cycles of birth, death, and rebirth brought these rural people a sense of their place in the cosmos, a timeless wisdom that urban people had supposedly lost. Germany, so the theory went, had to turn away from her mongrelized urban centers and rediscover her identity in her rural roots.

The ideology went further and held that this humble Volk actually stemmed from an ancient race of superior men, the Aryans, an ancient truth lost in the mists of time, but at last rediscovered. Now, after millennia, the Age of the Aryans was dawning. The humble Volk would be exalted and yes, the Aryans would once again rule over mankind, guided of course by the party.

This Volk, however, had to first decontaminate itself—return to its original Aryan purity if a Thousand-Year Reich was to flower. Just imagine where a purified Aryan race could lead the world if the country had the will to purify itself! The Nazi government had already legally forbidden interracial marriage. Mixing Aryans with lesser races brought about only genetic degeneration. In fact, Nazi researchers had traced most of Germany's medical and psychological ills—from hemophilia to schizophrenia—to mongrelized Aryan blood.

A program of euthanasia began within the Reich. Racial hygienists began selecting German mental patients for merciful executions. Inmates in mental institutions began quietly dying by carbon monoxide poisoning.

The Nazi regime was putting its ideology into practice.

A decade earlier, the Soviets had perfected their own machinery for mass execution of their own undesirables through a system of penal camps called the Gulag, through mass starvation of rebellious populations, and through a national network of prisons. These prisons resembled assembly lines, and included execution chambers with soundproof shooting galleries equipped with runnels for draining off blood, with mechanized hoists to remove bodies.

By the middle of the 1930s, this killing apparatus had dispatched so many Soviet citizens—many simply at random to reach arrest quotas—that a new social demographic appeared for the first time in Soviet society – *Dyeti byez prizornia* – that is, unattended orphans. These children usually begged in the streets and created a public relations nuisance for the Soviet regime when foreign dignitaries visited. Stalin eliminated this embarrassment by authorizing the execution of these orphans from the age of twelve.

The Soviet regime was also practicing its ideology.

THAT AFTERNOON, WINDS SWEPT IN ALONG THE eastern Carpathians, scattering and reforming the city's heaps of autumn leaves. Children dashed through the reddish whirlwinds, a real challenging day for bicycles. Steffie followed Theo through town into the Jewish quarter past the solitary synagogue, whose stepped roof echoed the ziggurats of the ancient Asian steppes. They sped past dog packs patrolling Kalush's central market, and then pedaled hard to climb up to the Polish quarter with its rows of baroque houses, each with a balcony resting on braces like entwined olive branches, a refinement now out of place in the stagnant economy of 1939.

They stopped to survey the city's northern outskirts and its row of breweries, some still operating despite the worldwide depression that had crippled Poland, the weeds threatening now to overgrow the railroad spurs from the warehouses. Steffie fought to catch her breath, while Theo cast a wary eye across the overgrown fields for thieves, glowing cigarette butts often giving them away. He turned to the northwest and scanned the horizon. "What are you thinking about?" she asked.

"The storm that's coming our way."

"How much time do you think we have?"

"Probably by the end of the week."

They reached the town's highest point. The Wozniak's sprawling white clapboard house came into view, to Theo, almost like an exposed artillery target. Starlings had gathered for migration over the roof, perching on fences and ignoring the scarecrows in the medicinal garden. Their enemies, bluish-gray sparrow hawks, began circling above, as the starlings' outer sentries screeched for an early departure.

"Don't worry about my family," Steffie said as they rested their handlebars against the porch railing. "They're actually looking to you for guidance."

Theo saw his mother-in-law open the door a crack and beam at her firstborn daughter. Maria Wozniak had always reminded him of a mournful virgin icon; in fact, like all the Wozniaks, with their large, liquid eyes, elongated noses, and generous lips. How could he win her over now? He bowed, brushing his lips past her arthritic knuckles. She raised her hand until he straightened.

He looked for Viktor, but Steffie's sister quickly stepped forward in her yellow, Roaring-Twenties-style blouse, her golden hair center-parted, her closely set, blue-gray eyes unblinking, searching, lip-reading. She reached out to hug him. "I knew the Germans wouldn't dare shoot a handsome dog like you," Zosia said, slurring her words as usual. The same epidemic that had eliminated his own sense of smell as a child had also left Zosia nearly deaf. But Zosia's spirit astonished him – her refusal to let her near deafness hold her back. She must have decided to compensate, Theo thought, by becoming the most helpful and giving person in Kalush, if not all Galicia.

Behind her, Theo saw a houseful of relatives and guests.

Theo's father-in-law stepped in. "Can I claim the war hero for a moment before you monopolize him?" He led Theo by the arm into the family library, into the company of his well-worn European classics. "We learned about your unit—about a third of them Ukrainian," Anton Wozniak began. "You know, I still recall the sound of the first bullets whistling past my head in the Great War. As an officer, how would you rate the German army?"

Theo's mind flashed on a horse staggering in its own entrails. He forced himself to refocus. "Their army?" he repeated. "Professional—very professional."

"And their tactics? As effective as in the Great War?"

Theo briefly closed his eyes. His father-in-law lowered his voice. "You must have gone through a baptism of fire out there," he said, touching Theo's shoulder.

"How can I put it?" Theo began. "You know all of that celebrated German genius—Beethoven, Bach."

"Yes, Goethe, Leibnitz, Schiller."

"Well, that genius is fully focused now—"

"On warfare, on conquest. Exactly! Who even knows if the Poles could have prepared adequately to face them," Wozniak said, squinting and gliding a finger across the spines of his German tomes. "In fact, who knows if anyone in Europe can, now that the Germans have set their minds to it." Theo noticed that in profile, Anton Wozniak, with his handlebar moustache and rumpled pompadour, looked exactly like Friedrich Nietzsche, but he had heard that unlike Nietzsche, the great German philosopher, his father-in-law had returned to Christianity – but only after some horrifying, life-changing event.

"This time, the Poles acted stupidly," Wozniak went on. "Particularly that colonel, that would-be emperor, trying to play the hero between Hitler and Stalin." He opened a historical atlas to a dog-eared page. "After the Miracle of the Vistula, the Poles could have recognized our independence and had all of Ukraine with them as an ally. Imagine! A buffer against Russia! And what did they get instead?" He tapped an energetic finger on a map. Theo read the large block letters: The Third Partition of Poland—1795, Poland Eradicated from the Map of Europe. Wozniak shut the book. "Who would have believed history repeating so soon after Poland's independence."

"Another partition!"

"And in the middle of all of that, you survived a German ambush, capture, and you maneuvered back through occupied territory. Heroic!"

"I really don't believe anything I did was heroic."

"Keeping a cool head through such constant danger—nothing short of heroic."

Theo looked up to see his mother-in-law in the doorway. How long had she been watching? "The Lord saw fit to save you," she said, "and for that, we're grateful."

"Thank you," Theo said.

"What about Panasevich's boy?" she asked.

"Panko?" Theo said. "Now there was a hero, a true hero."

"You should visit his mother and tell her personally," she said. "Come. We're ready."

 THE FALL OF THE POLISH STATE WAS ABOUT to introduce the peoples of eastern Europe to two conquerors with radically different approaches to government, each with its own ideology, each breaking with Western tradition, and each considering itself pioneering and "scientific"; one ideology coming at them from the east, and the other from the west.

The National Socialist regime in Germany believed that it had to cleanse society of "genetic impurity" to achieve their vision of an earthly utopia: a new society of racially pure Aryans who would rule over Europe and humanity. The Communist regime, on the other hand, believed that if it eliminated undesirable social classes in its midst that an entirely new, conflict-free society would emerge—and usher in the Communist vision of an earthly utopia.

Ukrainian villagers, accustomed to periodic political upheavals, and unsure which rumors to believe, began preparing for the triumphal entry of either of the two conquerors; some villages erecting ten-meter high welcome arches, with *Herzliches Willkommen* in German on one side—complete with swastikas—and *Dobro Pozhalovat'* in Russian on the other side, complete with hammers and sickles.

STEFFIE AND ZOSIA WERE LOADING THE LINEN-COV-
ered table with the choicest Galician specialties: steaming cabbage
rolls, potato-and-cheese dumplings, assortments of cold cuts arranged
into interlocking floral designs, pickled herring in brine, a bowl of
blood-red beets grated with horseradish, and a bluish-white ingot of
salo, or pork fatback, a rural staple from Theo's childhood. He didn't
much care, however, for the thinly sliced cucumber crumpled in its
own juice, aptly named *miseria*. Pitchers of stewed fruit *kompot* sim-
mered next to a bottle of honey vodka. He knew a four-layer Viennese
torte would follow it all, each layer with its own icing.

"I'll light the candles, Zosia," Mrs. Wozniak called out. "Just bring
the *Studynets'* up from the basement!"

The main dish, shredded pork in chilled gelatin, looked to Theo like
a sawed-out section of a frozen lake with minnows and frogs trapped
beneath the surface, but he loved it, especially with a little vinegar.

But the Wozniaks couldn't keep producing extravagant spreads like
this much longer, Theo knew. Poland's collapse would bring in shortages.
He remembered the ever-hungry armies passing through Hadynkivtsi—
Russians, Germans, Austrians—each invader requisitioning first the
eggs, then the family's poultry, then the cattle, and finally the winter
supplies of pickled cabbage and smoked sausage, paying at first, and then
seizing it outright. He remembered toward the war's end when his gaunt
mother had uncovered a single slice of moldy bread forgotten in a draw-
er. She'd broken it and shared it; his hunger overcoming his revulsion.

Steffie took her assigned seat to Theo's right, and to his left, he
felt Katrusia's presence. Lovely Katrusia, as everyone called Slavko's
fiancée, whose complexion and ebony eyes, other women surely tried
to imitate with makeup; but also Katrusia, the singer and musician,
whose fingers skipped like elves across the keys. "We couldn't afford
to lose another accomplished musician," she whispered. "Welcome
back." Theo breathed easier seeing Slavko across from her. His

brother-in-law spoke softly, groomed modestly, and dressed – well, he dressed like a store clerk, yet who didn't respect him? Who didn't appreciate the sense of welcome he naturally extended to everyone he met? Theo just worried that one day some ruthless woman would exploit his open-hearted nature – should he ever lose his own open-hearted Katrusia.

"Did you hear the last broadcast on the shortwave?" Anton Wozniak said. "The Germans are evacuating L'viv." He nodded to Theo. "We're all eager to hear your impressions from the front—your prognosis."

"It's already getting dark," his wife complained and noted that for some reason her son Vlodko had still not arrived from his church in the hills of Tysmenichany.

"That's a bit worrying," Anton Wozniak said, "Alright, then, I'll have to do the benediction in his place. Welcome … welcome to our moment of peace. May the Lord watch over our family," he began as they all stood. "A time of trials awaits us, and we must prepare ourselves." He looked out over the table. "Each of us at this table has a special responsibility! We've all defied the odds and completed university, marking all of us here as the intelligentsia, the leaders in our community."

"Leaders? Or do you mean targets?" someone echoed hoarsely. A short, wiry man tottered down the dark hallway, trying to fend off Zosia with his free hand. "I can walk by myself," he croaked in a voice almost too faint to recognize, and reached the table and looked up. Theo didn't immediately recognize Viktor Sabat. His brother-in-law looked less like the handsome man the Poles had arrested in the spring and more like some defeated Mongol invader, sunken cheeks and a scabby scalp in place of the mop of hair. His hands were trembling.

"How in God's holy name did you slip out of Bereza?" Theo said. "I thought the Russians had overrun all of Belarus."

"Viktor spent seven days without food and water, "Zosia interjected. "When he got here, his gums had swelled from starvation! Did you know gums can bleed—even on milk-soaked bread?"

"Starvation, we saw too much of it in the Great War," Anton Wozniak said. "Pour him a drink. Theo, you should hear his story."

Viktor explained how less than two weeks ago, back in the Bereza prison, the guards had marched the Ukrainian prisoners out for execution. The commandant ordered the guards to raise their carbines and fire. "Do you know what the body does at the moment of execution when the guards just shoot over your head? For some reason, the commandant changed his mind. They locked us up again, and then—abandoned us without food or water. The people in town heard us yelling day and night. It took them a week before they came and broke the locks."

"The hand of fate," Anton Wozniak said. "If the Russians had arrived a day earlier, they'd have shot every Ukrainian prisoner in there." He poured out measures of honey vodka.

Viktor said that after their escape, the Polish and Ukrainian prisoners split up; his group of Ukrainians slogged south through the Pripet Swamps for days, until they emerged and ran into the German army.

"But you were unarmed," Theo said.

"Exactly," Viktor said. "We debated for an hour, and then chose a delegation to ask if we could join them. We told the Germans that we just needed weapons to help them drive the Russians out of Ukraine. We would fight alongside them."

"See," Zosia broke in. "He wasn't thinking clearly. He already wanted to fight—in his condition!"

"The Germans listened politely, offered us our first hot meal, and then told us"—he struggled to form the German words—"'Wir brauchen euch nicht.'"

"We don't need you," Theo translated.

66

This German rejection of Ukrainian volunteers sparked a back-and-forth across the table about Germany's intentions, with Slavko asking if the Germans thought they could take on Moscow by themselves, and Theo concluding, "The Germans didn't come to drive out the Russians. I saw that myself. They're definitely not here to help us."

"Absolutely right," Anton Wozniak agreed. "The Germans came to retake German territory from Poland, and to end Polish rule."

"As usual, we Ukrainians are caught between two fires," Maria Wozniak said.

"True! And we shall render unto Caesar what is Caesar's," Anton Wozniak said. "But remain true to yourselves." He held up his shot-glass. "Raise your glasses now to the inscrutable hand of Providence. Our young men, new family members both, have returned."

"To Providence!" Slavko agreed.

"And another excuse to drink," Mrs. Wozniak chided.

The men slammed their shot glasses down. The twenty-five watt overhead lightbulb brightened, flickered, and died.

"Maybe it's an omen!" Katrusia said.

Slavko pushed back his chair in the semidarkness and looked out the window. "The whole town's dark," he said.

Zosia set out a row of candles, each new flame casting shadows against the walls, until a flame illumined Katrusia, setting her braids aglow. "Should I tell you about a dream I had last week? Maybe a portent or maybe—" She paused and Slavko placed his hand over her open palm.

"Go on, child," Maria Wozniak said.

"In my dream, a storm came at us from across the plains, a silent storm," Katrusia continued. "But it almost tore the roofs off. It wasn't so much a nightmare, as a riddle. In my dreams animals sometimes talk. When the wind died down, I could see dogs outside running from house to house, warning us to stay inside."

"Talking dogs?" Steffie asked. "In what language?"

Katrusia's crystalline voice broke in laughter. "Well, maybe just a silly dream!"

"No," Maria Wozniak said, "the dream meant something."

"Or nothing at all," Steffie contradicted.

"Ah, dreams!" Anton Wozniak repeated, "I myself once dreamed of one world, believed in something called Pan-Slavism – Slavs of the world, unite!" he chuckled. "I thought we had so much to share – our cultures, our art, and our spirituality, yes, our special spirituality, which you hear in our music, our folksongs, unlike anything else in the world. But our neighbors cured me of my idealism. We'll never find common ground with them."

"How can we," Viktor agreed, "when Russians consider their harsh canine tongue superior to our own melodic Ukrainian which they consider an inferior dialect. 'Little Russian,' they call it. And the Poles – well they even have the gall to call our ancestral lands –"

"We all know," Maria Wozniak interrupted, "how they call it 'Little Poland.' It's getting chilly. 'Shouldn't we load the fireplace?" she said.

Zosia stood to help. "Tato, you saw Russians in the Great War," she said, "What should we do?"

"Somehow we will have to find a way to keep our schools," Slavko began, "our savings and loans," "our cooperative …"

"Slavko, as director," Katrusia said, "You know they'll come–"

"I can't abandon the cooperative," Slavko interrupted. "We'll just have to see how open they are to negotiation."

"But will the Communists even allow independent cooperatives," Katrusia continued.

Viktor was tapping his hands together, leaning forward. Steffie was picking at her plate, splitting the salad from the peas into two neat sections. "Those awful stories they tell about the Reds," she said, piercing the candlelight's hollow intimacy, "– the mass killings, the prisons

– maybe that's just–" she paused and looked at Slavko as if to find her bearings.

"Go on," Theo said, irritated. "Finish your thought."

"… You mean just propaganda?" Slavko whispered.

"Yes, I mean if a person joins the Communists," Steffie went one, "out of conviction, to create a better–"

"You're assuming, my dear Steffie," Mr. Wozniak broke in, "that after twenty years of purges, you can still find men in Russia guided by their conscience. Listen to me – all of you," He folded his hands together under his chin like a judge ready with a verdict. "Our best hope: We live in a constitutional democracy – yes, such as it is! The Russians cannot –"

A loud knock made them all turn toward the door.

"At last, my son Vlodko," Mrs. Wozniak said.

Anton Wozniak opened the door instead to a pale young man staring at them from under the visor of some sort of a military hat. In the semidarkness, Theo made out that the man wore a furazhka, a Red Army cap. The entire family arose in the candlelight to study this visitor, sporting a two-day stubble that shrouded a rigid jaw line.

"Greetings from the Committee of Workers and Peasants!" he announced in Russian, and tracked mud into the foyer.

"What kind of committee?" Anton Wozniak asked.

"The Soviet Army marches into Kalush tomorrow," he answered. "We expect revolutionary enthusiasm," the Soviet officer said. "Follow these instructions." He handed out mimeographed sheets and looked around the room until his eyes hit upon the corner icon, the Byzantine figures dark against the silver frame, and smirked. "And where's your pope?" he asked, using the derogatory slang for "priest."

"My son, you mean?" Anton Wozniak asked.

"You've got two bicycles outside," the visitor said. "Why do you need more than one?"

 THOUGH WORLD WAR I HAD SPAWNED half a dozen new countries out of the ruins of the old European empires, an independent Ukraine did not emerge. Defeated in battle, western Ukraine came under the newly created state of Poland, while eastern Ukraine, after prolonged fighting, found itself reunited again to Russia.

The Communists had held on to power in Russia. But the revolution had failed to take root beyond the borders of old imperial Russia, though Stalin was not a man to admit defeat. Outwitting his rivals, he emerged as general secretary of the newly proclaimed Soviet Union.

First order of business: protect the Communist victory, and build Socialism first in one country – the USSR; and of equal importance, instill some discipline into the rebellious Ukrainians. He would punish their tendency toward "separatism" with the most massive genocide history had yet seen.

Many western Ukrainians knew of Stalin forcing collectivization in eastern Ukraine, ordering farmers to abandon their farms and to join government-run collectives. The Bolsheviks launched the nationalization of farms by first disarming the Ukrainian countryside, confiscating the peasantry's personal weapons, and then by banishing the most productive farmers to Siberia and publicly executing any outspoken dissenters. The Red Army then cordoned off the independent-minded nation, while Moscow began demanding ever-increasing deliveries of wheat—with instant execution as the punishment for pilfering even a single stalk. The many uprisings, all uncoordinated in an era before mass communications, died on the vine. A third of the countryside finally starved to death in the winter of 1932-1933. To replace them, Stalin simply imported Russian settlers and other nationalities he found more subservient.

Despite reports of the genocide leaking to the West, many western Ukrainians simply refused to believe that a Socialist government—any Socialist government—could so brutally mistreat its own citizens.

Theo's father, Stefan Diachok,
circa 1910

Theo's mother, Evdoksia
Prockiw, circa 1920

Theodosius ("Theo") Diachok, 1935,
Chortkiv, Ukraine

Theo with his 4th grade pupils, Veldizh,
Ukraine, 1938

Theo with 2nd Lieutenant Panasevich, fellow
Ukrainian infantry officer in the Polish Army.
July 26, 1936

In addition to painting, Theo did sculpture …

… and caused quite a sensation with
his caricatures of his college mates at
L'viv Pedagogical Institute

Steffie's father, Anton Wozniak, circa 1927

Steffie with her mother, Maria, of the Korol family. Kalush, 1934

Steffie Wozniak in a "Flapper" hairdo. Circa 1932

Steffie rode her bike great distances to teach villagers Ukrainian grammar and embroidery – at a time when the Polish government was shutting down Ukrainian schools and Polonizing the countryside. Circa 1938, Kalush, Ukraine

Steffie loved the magical world of children and took her pupils on imaginative outings and taught them animal lore. Kalush, September 18, 1938

Steffie with a few of her "12 admirers." Though she dated the brother of Stepan Bandera, the OUN leader, she preferred the UNDO's program. Kalush, Easter of 1939

Joseph Stalin, cigarette in hand, greets Hitler's Foreign Minister, Joachim von Ribbentrop to negotiate the Non-Aggression Treaty, Moscow, August 28, 1939

Adolf Hitler with Stalin's Foreign Minister, Vycheslav Molotov. The Führer attempted to convince his archrival the Soviet Union that, after carving up Eastern Europe between them, he had no more territorial designs.

The Red Army displays its finest in L'viv in September 1939. In smaller towns the march-in elicited more unintended shock than awe – at Soviet destitution.

After occupying Eastern Poland, the Soviets prepared the population for annexation. Here Ukrainian schoolchildren appear in a "spontaneous" demonstration demanding "Stalin's Constitution" for the occupied territories.

Steffie with sister Zosia Kalush, Ukraine circa 1938

Steffie's brother, Rev. Volodymvr ("Vlodko") Wozniak, Kalush, 1939

Steffie's brother Slavko Wozniak 1939

Zosia and Viktor Kalush, Summer 1939

Theo and Steffie during their courtship, Kalush, 1939

THE OCCUPATION

On the morning of the Red Army's march-in, Mr. Wozniak over-ruled his wife's objections. She wanted to arrive late and wait quietly and unnoticed at the crowd's outskirts. He insisted they come early instead to get a clean view to better assess their new occupiers. Slavko agreed—no one would suspect the front row of spectators of anti-Soviet views.

The Wozniaks crowded together on the sidewalk along Market Street, Kalush's ancient thoroughfare. Theo felt needlessly exposed and vulnerable, as if a well-aimed shell would terminate him together with the whole Wozniak clan. An irrational fear, or just post-battle nerves? Maybe he'd just heard too many unconfirmed rumors about the Russian Revolution's bloody history.

Theo watched a brawny man stand upright at the intersection and yank the reins of his country wagon. Two boys clambered out to claim a place along the crowded curb; men in visor caps or Homburg hats, the women in head scarves or stylish hats. Theo recognized the post-master across the road, and—could it be?—yes, the postmaster's son, his most troublesome pupil.

"Ignore that woman waving at us," Steffie whispered. "I know that busybody from teacher's college." Theo glimpsed a thickset young woman in one of those feathered bowler hats, regrettably in style now, and dutifully looked away. He watched two nuns across the road, like a pair of bookends, supervising a row of teenaged schoolgirls with high socks and pleated skirts, and next to them, Theo recognized the seventeen-year-old twins – the Pride of Kalush, some people called them – a brother and sister – both gifted singers, folk dancers, and the town's most envied youth organizers – the two as stately as altar candles, Theo thought, and as perishable. All the spectators looked east, shielding their eyes, and, as instructed, all of them wore red ribbons fluttering from their lapels.

Inspectors in civilian clothes with red armbands began strutting along the street and, with military bearing, motioning the onlookers back onto the curb. A pair approached. The shorter one stopped and pointed to Theo's boots. "Former Polish officer?" he asked in Russian, and looked at his colleague, who asked for identification papers.

A careless mistake, even stupid, Theo realized—good-quality leather boots obviously commanded the Russians' full attention. As his ID booklet left his fingers, Theo felt all feeling drain from his legs. The taller inspector flipped the booklet open with one hand. "A teacher," he read. "One of those western Ukrainian family names—Diachok."

"Church cantor," the shorter one said with a grin, and reached up and pinched Theo's red ribbon in his fingers. "Don't we need a cantor at headquarters?" he said, and jerked the bow loose, the two ends falling limp.

The taller one smiled. "*Da, on budyet nam pyet'. Zapisat' familiyu.*" (Yes, we must have him over to sing for us. Jot down his name.)

The inspectors strode off toward the nuns and schoolgirls across the road.

Theo felt Steffie's hand clasping his fingers. "What did that mean, you'll sing for them?" she whispered.

Didn't Steffie know the euphemism? "Just their form of humor," Theo assured his wife.

"Just humor, you think?" Theo heard an eastern Ukrainian accent behind him. "No, they'll remember you now."

Theo turned to confront gray eyes magnified behind thick glasses perched on a slender nose.

"You're with the Wozniak family," the man volunteered. "Who wouldn't know the Wozniaks in Kalush?"

"Your name?" Mr. Wozniak pressed.

"Moskalenko, but that's not important," the easterner whispered, and leaned forward. "I know these people."

Did this man escape from eastern Ukraine? Theo wondered. Or did he arrive with the regime?

"Moskalenko," Mr. Wozniak repeated. "You're not the Kiev correspondent?"

"I didn't think our newspapers reached this far," the easterner replied.

A motorized clamor arose down the street. A haze of diesel fumes rose through the yellowed poplars, and mechanical shapes appeared against the morning sky, with black-helmeted figures protruding, their clenched fists raised. Little red flags began obediently fluttering along the lines of spectators. Tank treads prattled, then clanged against the pavement.

The tank column approached. Theo recognized old T-26 tanks from his training, their peculiar small-caliber cannons and broad, flat, protective skirts just begging, he thought, for one or two tungsten-tipped anti-tank rockets. "Like cockroaches from hell," Steffie whispered.

A group of young men rushed from the crowd, to Theo's astonishment, and threw bouquets at the tanks, some running alongside and kissing the hot metal. Who were these oddities welcoming the

Soviets? Theo thought. Then he recognized them by their clothes: recent Jewish escapees from German-occupied Poland.

"They think they're greeting their liberators," Theo heard the easterner say.

An armored car grated into view with two helmeted soldiers balanced atop, distributing flyers. Some in the crowd broke ranks to grab the sheets of paper billowing through the air. Theo stooped to pick up a flyer. *Printed in good, grammatical Ukrainian*, he conceded. A third soldier shouted into a bullhorn, "We have come to empower you to take back your country! To break the chains of your Polish landowners! And now greet your liberator, the Red Army!"

The strains of a marching band reached them. Theo was expecting the stirring Communist march, "The Internationale," or maybe some Russian march, but instead he recognized a familiar Polish cavalry tune. The Reds had clearly worked out the propaganda angle. Rows of nearly antique, long rifles with fixed bayonets caught his eye, and then shiny, knee-high boots that mysteriously didn't bend. *Ah, plastic boots,* Theo realized. *Not even leather.* He heard that the Red Army only distributed leather boots for actual combat. Yet other marchers tramped by with dark cloth of some kind wrapped tightly around their feet. The coats varied in length, and most needed patching.

They strutted on, no one single ethnicity dominating, even the sallow complexions from the Asian republics appearing among the hard, angular, hungry Russian faces, their jaws jutting, their plastic boots kicking upwards, their eyes glowing, but with what? With some sort of pride as liberators? Or was it embarrassment? Were these impoverished marchers already too stunned, Theo thought, on seeing Kalush's fashionable clothes and well-fed children to act out their charade as liberators? Could they already sense how comical their barnyard strutting appeared?

The crowd's excitement tapered to silence, as if witnessing the March of the Have-nots. Theo heard Slavko ask the easterner if the Soviet regime permitted cooperatives, just as a truck carrying the only smartly-dressed soldiers sped by.

"Cooperatives?" Moskalenko chuckled. "You mean independent cooperatives?" He looked at Slavko askance and nodded toward the street. "See those soldiers right there in the peaked caps?" he whispered. "They're the ones who'll start deporting people to Siberia. You think they'll permit cooperatives?"

Mr. Wozniak shook his head. "They won't dare try that sort of thing here," he retorted. "This isn't the Donbass! They've stumbled into a civilized part of Europe."

The columns rolled on, the tank drivers' fists raised.

 IN DECLARING THEMSELVES THE "FLAG-bearers of high humanitarian principles," the Soviets initially vowed to rescue their "brothers," the Ukrainians, as well as the Belarusians, from their Polish overlords. The first Soviet actions struck a chord in Ukrainian hearts, and initially turned many of Ukrainians into supporters.

The Poles had earlier shut down hundreds of Ukrainian-language schools in the 1930s in their drive to consolidate their newly formed country into one nation, with one common language, with one interpretation of history. The new regime reopened these shuttered schools. The Poles had also promised in the Versailles Treaty to establish a Ukrainian-language university in the regional capital city of L'viv, but dragged their heels for two decades. The new regime immediately opened L'viv University, long a stronghold of Polish culture, to

Ukrainian students and professors, and declared Ukrainian, a formerly despised "peasant dialect," its official language of instruction.

The new regime also opened up a network of health clinics throughout the rural areas, where most Ukrainians actually lived.

But it was in land ownership that the new regime demonstrated perhaps the strongest apparent commitment to reform. The Poles, though in the minority in western Ukraine, had owned the majority of the land. The new Soviet regime seized sprawling Polish estates and began redistributing half of their land, free of charge, to landless Ukrainian peasants. And to complete the reallocation, the regime began expelling the two hundred thousand Polish settlers who had taken over Ukrainian lands in the same drive to "Polonize" western Ukraine, and returned much of their land to the previous Ukrainian owners.

While these apparent reforms were winning over more and more Ukrainian hearts and minds, exactly as earlier Soviet promises had won over Russia's peasants and workers during the Russian Revolution, the Soviet secret police began secretly fanning out throughout western Ukraine, gathering names, with the aim of closing down resurgent Ukrainian cultural institutions, like *Prosvita* (Enlightenment) and the Shevchenko Scientific Society. Local Communists who had welcomed the new regime's arrival began quietly working with the People's Commissariat for Internal Affairs (NKVD) to "unmask" local leaders and nationalists, and to mark them for eventual arrest.

THEO HURRIED ACROSS TOWN DURING HIS LUNCH BREAK, and found Slavko bent forward at his desk, the phone pressed to his ear. A portrait of a disapproving Stalin had already replaced a *Buy Ukrainian* poster on the pale green wall over Slavko's desk. "Glad you came so quickly," Slavko whispered, "Family emergency." He cupped the phone. "The Red Army came yesterday, looking for Viktor."

"To induct him?" Theo asked and sat.

Slavko swiveled back toward the window. "No, no, Mister Minister, you have my full attention," he said into the receiver. "We've been hiring mainly Ukrainians, simply because the Polish government kept Ukrainians out of the work force. No other reason . . . no, no, Poles and Jews have had their own sources of employment." Slavko nodded repeatedly, as if conceding a point across a negotiating table. "I can assure you, we've *always* paid close attention to ethnic balance. ... Yes, both on the workforce and on the board."

Theo had only spoken once or twice by telephone, and found the metallic voice somehow strident, and cold. He wondered how Slavko stayed so calm defending MasloSoyuz into that shiny brass receiver. He thought of the Russians on the other end as aggressive and cagey but knew that Slavko always thought a few steps ahead of any adversary. How else could anyone succeed in the stormy, multi-ethnic cauldron called Galicia?

"Another minority board member?" Slavko was saying. "Of course, I welcome it, but who'll pay his salary?" Finally, he cradled the receiver and faced Theo. "Now they're trying to bring in their own auditors – you understand, Theo – so they can cook the books and appropriate all they like from our farms, just like their apparatchiks do in eastern Ukraine. I know their game." He glanced at his watch. "How much time do you have left, Theo?"

"Not quite ten minutes."

"The new Soviet policy for the working man," Slavko said. "What is it now? Ten minutes late for work, a year in prison?"

Theo smiled wryly. "Our first taste of the workers' paradise. You said the Red Army wants to take Viktor, but why now in his condition?"

"I wonder if they even know what condition he's in, or that he just escaped from Bereza." Slavko leaned forward. "But I'm thinking of Zosia's condition, too," he said. "Theo, is a child ever born into this world at an opportune time?"

"Your sister's expecting?" Theo asked.

"Think of the joy that should could bring … should bring." Slavko leaned in further and whispered, "You know what Zosia told the Red Army recruiters yesterday? That she hadn't seen Viktor in months and that he never returned from the war." Theo whistled. "Well, of course they searched every room in the house, even the woodshed. They said they'd be back."

Theo imagined how long an outspoken anti-Communist like Viktor would last in the Red Army. Eventually Viktor would blurt something out. And as soon as the NKVD got hold of Viktor's Polish arrest records—and found out he belonged to the OUN—Viktor would face arrest, torture to reveal his contacts, and then a well-placed pistol shot to the back of the head.

"Time's not on our side," Slavko said. "All it takes is one informant, one nasty neighbor."

"And there goes Zosia, too," Theo added.

By now they all knew how the Soviet regime treated the wives of anyone arrested under Article 58, Counter-revolutionary Activity, or the famous Article 57, Anti-Soviet Agitation. The State sentenced the wives to ten years at hard labor – hauling wheelbarrows or chopping lumber in the subzero Arctic – for the crime of having married an "enemy of the people."

The door opened to the sudden clacking of typewriters. A young woman, hair parted into two silky blond pompadours, handed Slavko a document and indulgently watched as her boss mumbled some numbers from the columns of statistics while sliding beads across the abacus perched on his desk. "Try as they might, the Poles couldn't force us into bankruptcy," Slavko said at last, shaking his head. "But this regime, with their commissars –"

The young woman parted her lips as if to say something comforting, perhaps a prayer, but quietly closed the door. "You speak very openly around her," Theo said.

"I trust her." Slavko said and glanced at his watch and folded his large hands together. He looked steadily into Theo's eyes. "But I don't know if we've earned your trust," he said, "if I have even the right to ask you this – to put yourself at risk for our family – especially when, quite frankly, you and Steffie," he said and paused, "are still working things out. And, and I'm sure you're aware of my mother's – well, her resistance to you, which I hope you don't take too seriously. You know, no suitor was ever good enough for her daughter." He looked steadily into Theo's eyes and continued, "So, I don't know if you will ever really consider yourself part of our family." Theo looked down, feeling unmasked. "But whatever you decide," Slavko concluded, "personally, I will still think the world of you."

Slavko's words painfully confirmed his outsider status. Honestly, did he see himself part of the Wozniak family? Had he ever felt himself part of any family, for that matter, even his own fractured family? For a moment the scene he had long suppressed flashed in his mind – the snowed in cottage in Hadynkivtsi – the night the blizzard had reached the window, climbing through the night, climbing until the snow solidly blocked the doors and muted God's light as the day dawned – while the gangrene, which no one could arrest, had swollen from his mother's hand, climbing along her arm up toward her face – the day that changed his life forever and made him into a vagabond, a child adrift, searching until this day for some order, for a connection.

He remembered her last words, "What will become of you, my three children?" Yet during the tragedy he had felt only an indifference, as if watching inept community theater – in fact, like the disconnection he had felt marching through the German crossfire.

As Slavko's sympathetic eyes scanned his face for clues, Theo understood he had to choose – to fully enter the Wozniak family, or to stay clear. Theo looked through the plate glass at the row of idle MasloSoyuz trucks, standing at the curb. "So, you want me to hide Viktor," he concluded.

"Can you do it, Theo?" Slavko said. "Yes, it's a risk, but we've got to get him out of Kalush by tomorrow morning. I would do it myself, but they're beginning to watch my every move."

Theo firmly replaced the teacup. "So exactly where should I take him?" he asked.

"Uncle Wozniak's farm."

"Your Uncle Wozniak? Seriously? Isn't he—"

"He's family," Slavko interjected, "our family." Slavko paused and checked his watch. "You have to get back. By the way, Theo, how's your job now? Stable?"

"Oh, about as stable as yours, Slavko. No, listen: transporting Viktor that distance, in his condition . . . it's quite far, and if we manage to get through the checkpoints, I somehow can't imagine Uncle Wozniak agreeing to hide Viktor." Slavko stood up.

"It *is* far," Slavko agreed, "but that's exactly what we need."

Theo studied Slavko's intense gray eyes transparent somehow as two pools of rainwater.

STALIN WAS STILL DECIDING WHAT TO DO with the tens of thousands of Polish Officer POWs he had amassed. One hint of their possible fate came from Marxist theory.

Communists considered their revolution an international movement, one without boundaries. Therefore, bourgeois conventions on how to treat POWs simply did not apply to them. Any opposing officers falling into their hands became fair game for court martial—not as prisoners of war, but as counterrevolutionaries—if these officers could not be persuaded to join the revolution. Otherwise, eliminating these influential bourgeois nationalists clearly advanced the worldwide revolution.

For their part, captured Polish officers wondered why the Russians held them as POWs, since Russia had never declared war on Poland. The captured Polish officers didn't seem to grasp their status as potential enemies of the revolution, subject to the party's whims.

In the middle of the fall of 1939, NKVD officers began conducting lengthy interrogations of the Polish officers, including Theo's captured colleagues, now concentrated in four camps and prisons throughout the USSR. The NKVD couched the deadly serious interviews in friendly terms, such as, "If I were passing through your home town, would you invite me in for a cup of tea?" Polish officers, believing themselves protected under the Geneva Convention, answered honestly.

"ONCE YOU GET TO THE FARM," ZOSIA MURMURED, "stay put, or they'll catch you and throw you in prison again. You want to eat undercooked buckwheat again, mixed with sand?"

"But Zosia," Viktor said, and encircled her tighter, "the sand helped me chew through the bugs. I got used to it."

She pushed him back. "All right, then I'll start cooking roaches with your kasha," she said, tapping him on the cheek. "But no more heroics! You're my hero, and that's enough for you, okay? Think of our baby."

Viktor nuzzled her. "Picked a name yet?" he asked.

Feeling like a voyeur, Theo turned away, impatient to get going. Slavko had insisted they leave in the dead of night, with most of the militia still passed out drunk.

"'Roman,' if it's a boy," Theo heard Zosia's husky whisper. "And 'Roma,' if a girl."

"And if it's a cherub?" Viktor asked.

"Then I'll name him after you."

They found the stallion limping badly, so they had to reconfigure the carriage steering, the brow band, the collar tug—all of it—for their only other horse, a filly barely three-year-old.

At the gray of sunrise, Slavko helped a pale and dizzy Viktor mount the tailboard. Theo found the peasant hat extending over Viktor's ears comical, as bad as the dung-stained boots meant to disguise them as farmers if trouble came calling. Slavko cracked the door open to a blast of light, as Viktor winced. Zosia threw her arms around his neck. "Don't do anything stupid!" she cried.

"Zosia, please, no tears."

The carriage lurched into the bite of November. "I'll pray for you every hour!" Zosia called.

"Good!" Viktor yelled back. "And practice all the commandments for me, too!" He turned to Theo. "Will I get along all right with this uncle? What if he finds out I'm with the Nationalists?"

"Would that be so bad?"

"He's a Communist!"

Theo knew only too well about the recent rash of assassinations between Nationalists and Communists. "They're family," Theo said. "And you know, blood is thicker than water."

"Family? Blood? That's supposed to reassure me?"

"Why were you just so flippant with Zosia about religion?"

"Religion? I've learned enough about religion in prison. It stared me in the face every day. The Poles pray to their virgin, and then happily beat us half to death, and we pray to our own virgin and fight back and kill them if we could. And where's God in all this? A spectator, enjoying the fight?"

"Your theology needs some work. Viktor, somehow I'm not surprised how you always get into trouble," Theo sighed. "How did you survive those months in solitary?"

"You seriously want to know, Theo? Well, alright, it may help you one day if they nab you too. First thing: develop a routine, or you'll go crazy; like, regular exercise every day. Roman told me to focus my mind; constantly work my memory. I tried to recite every poem I ever learned by heart. And I tried to identify and examine every single month of my life. The worst thing was half rations. You somehow get used to a total fast, but half rations make you obsess for food. It helped me to think about Zosia, in fact, I thought of her a lot!"

"Must have been weird, knowing the guards were looking in."

In Kalush's main square, Polish- and Yiddish-language signs still covered the first and second floors of the buildings, free-market advertising in blue, red, and black for everything from dietetic table water, legal services, to cut-rate Parisian fashions, but the storefronts had gone nearly empty, despite the throngs of shoppers. "Look at those poor souls trying to feed their families, probably waiting half the night," Theo said.

"Zosia was in line at the butcher yesterday. Those commissars came in and just cleared out the shelves with their new currency. Know what she came back with? A bag of, ah, Theo –" Viktor waved his hand. "You don't want to know."

Shoppers kept coming, forming lines that began snaking around street corners. "We're quickly becoming fully Soviet," Viktor went on. "Heard this one from eastern Ukraine, '*Ні корови, ні свині – тільки Сталін на стіні*.'? [No pig in the pen, no cow in the stall, just Stalin's portrait on the wall.]

Theo pulled the reins hard, as men with red armbands and guns strapped around their coats appeared and spread out along the sidewalk. A shrill police whistle made the filly bolt into the intersection. Theo yanked her back. A militiaman shook his fist at Theo and turned his attention to a procession of horse-drawn carts rolling into the square, each loaded down with pyramids of pumpkins and potatoes, the drivers in embroidered peasant shirts. Above each driver, a hand-painted sign read "We joyfully deliver our harvest to the Communist Party!"

"Inspiring, isn't it?" Viktor said.

As the procession passed, they saw the accordionists, feet dangling from the back, each grinning like a cadaver churning out the same village wedding song. Children ran behind, as if hoping for a stray pumpkin or potato to bounce out of the carts – the shoppers clutching their bags observed the scene transfixed.

A pair of militiamen approached the carriage. "Common criminals," Viktor whispered, and pulled up his backpack. "Six weeks ago, behind bars, and now, high and mighty!" Theo noticed Viktor's fingers reflexively patting a bulge in the backpack. So, Viktor had packed a pistol!

"Give them our best backcountry accents," Theo whispered. "But let me do the talking."

One militiaman grabbed the horse's bit. The other demanded documents. "Comrade," Viktor drawled, and winked at the hungover face. "Don't tell me you're still too drunk to recognize your fellow working men?" Theo saw Viktor reach into his backpack. "I'm sure though that you'll find this document acceptable." Viktor said and slipped a bottle into the militiaman's coat, who grinned and waved them on, out of town. Yes, Theo thought, Viktor picked up some impressive street smarts in prison – hopefully enough to behave at the farm.

From the last of Kalush's seven hills, an open countryside of wheat and alfalfa stretched out before them – a glowing scene with the sun at their back, one just begging for a free afternoon for his canvas and paints; but he also knew that close by in those same hills too stood a tidy homestead that his father-in-law had once gambled away.

At midday, they needed to rest the filly, and Viktor asked to stop at one village that stood out for its line of sprawling Poplars. Theo began drawing water from a well, as Viktor shouldered his pack. Viktor was about to jump off the carriage, when Theo casually said, "You've been out of action for half a year, Viktor. What if the Soviets infiltrated the OUN, and you walk into a trap?"

Viktor balanced against the buckboard for a moment, as if another dizzy spell had hit him and crouched back down.

Theo realized he had guessed right, that Viktor wanted to rejoin the Ukrainian resistance. "Viktor," he said, "you do know, don't you, that some men would kill for what you already have – right under your nose."

"Really?" Viktor said and straightened up, "And exactly what is it I already have?"

"A woman," Theo said and sighed deeply, "a woman who loves you." He regarded Viktor's gray eyes peering back from under the straw rim, and added, "You have someone faithful to you, makes a home for you. Do you how many men have tasted that, lost it, and would give anything to have it back?" Theo handed him the bucket. "Where do you think patriotism begins, Viktor – if not at home," he said, "with Zosia – yes, with pregnant, little Zosia."

Viktor took a couple of gulps and turned his glance to the white-washed village houses, their yards full of poppies and sunflowers. "I miss my prison friends, "he said. "Men like Martyniuk, Shukhevich, Bihun—best people I've ever known."

"Our time will come," Theo said. "We'll fight for our freedom one day, together, when the odds are right."

90

An hour before nightfall, the carriage approached an unruly little farm with an ancient windmill spinning in their direction.

 THE COMMUNIST REGIME BEGAN REVERS-ing itself in land ownership, without warning. Lands here and there expropriated from large Polish estates did not remain in Ukrainian hands for long. Formerly land-less peasants began surrendering their new land hold-ings, and were instead ordered to join a system of collective farms, where, bound to their land, they toiled purely for the state, the much-dreaded scheme in eastern Ukraine.

The new regime also began quietly restructuring urban society. Prominent western Ukrainian leaders began disappearing without a trace. The Soviets set to quietly deporting others for interrogation and for sentencing. Thousands suspecting themselves to be at risk tried fleeing across the border to the part of Poland that Germany now oc-cupied. The Communist regime also set to formally disbanding west-ern Ukraine's registered political parties. The democratically liberal UNDO, the party that had absorbed the labors of the Wozniaks and Theo and a million others, was about to shutter its doors for good. The mainstays of western Ukrainian society—Prosvita, Narodna Shkola, the cooperative movement; all developed painstakingly over decades against Polish opposition—now faced extinction, the end of civil soci-ety as western Ukrainians knew it.

But the Soviets took on a much more difficult target in attacking the OUN, an organization of hardened revolutionaries sworn to Ukraine's independence. Operating entirely underground, the OUN, by default, became western Ukraine's sole political force, and regrouped behind closed doors to take on a regime ten times more ruthless than Poland's.

Yet local Ukrainian Communists, still loyal to Marx's ideals of a class-less society, actively cooperated with the new regime to identify and turn over OUN members for arrest.

"A MAGICAL SETTING FOR A FARM," THEO SAID, IMAG-ining the right combination of pigments he'd squeeze onto a palette.

"Well, good forest for firewood for sure," Viktor said. "I wonder how this one Wozniak ended up here. I always took the Wozniaks for urban intellectuals, not farmers."

The filly trotted past a row of giant sunflowers tilting toward the retreating sun. A familiar melody drifted in. Women strolling four abreast through the harvested field were singing a folksong. A column of men in white muslin, carrying scythes, were ambling past the last of the rye, cut and rolled into millstone-sized bundles spaced about twenty meters apart.

Theo waved at the men, who paused as if trying to identity him, but didn't wave back.

Theo guided the carriage into the barnyard, scattering a commu-nity of chickens that noisily reconvened beneath a ladder. Light was shining from the adjacent barn.

They peered in. Two teenaged boys were swinging pitchforks at a trio of cows, their heads sunk into piles of hay. A woman lugged a pair of milk cans and stopped to gape, as did a gray-haired man, who grabbed his pitchfork and limped out of the shadows. "Ukrainians?" he asked.

"More than Ukrainians," Theo answered. "Relatives from the city."

"What a miracle, in-laws from the great metropolis of Kalush! In those clothes, I took you for Polish inspectors." He extended his soiled hand. "Wozniak," he said. "What brings you here?"

The woman lowered her milk cans. The filly sniffed her out-stretched hand and dropped her head. "She pulled you all the way?" she asked, massaging the twitching ears.

"We're in a bit of trouble and need your help." Theo said.

"Invite them in," the woman said.

Wozniak pointed to the well by the windmill where they could wash up.

"Ahh! Just what I miss about country life," Viktor sniggered, "the earthy smell of dung.".

"Reminds me," Theo said splashing a bucket over Viktor's dusty head. "Stay clear of the OUN and Stefan Bandera. Go ahead. I'll catch up."

Theo found the package Slavko had thrown together as a gift on the carriage's floorboard. He pulled the pistol from Viktor's pack, considered hiding it under the seat, but slid it instead under his belt. He looked up to survey the Podolian hills, their receding waves in silhouette now – their evening beauty fading fast into mystery, the very same hills of an ageless Ukrainian rhyme about a homeless orphan girl, a rhyme his aggrieved mother had often, perhaps even unconsciously recited. He groped his way through the semi-darkness into the farmhouse.

Light from the hearth lit up the entrance hallway; long wooden flails and rakes stood upright against one wall, and wooden ladles on cowhide strings hung on the other. A ledge held a collection of books. Yes, so these farmers read. Theo scanned their titles in the faint light: *Little Myron*, Franko's portrait of Ukrainian village life; *The Minstrel*, Shevchenko's collected poetry, resting against Marx's *Das Kapital*. He looked around, opened Marx's work, and began flipping pages until he found a bookmark halfway in. He tried to decipher the Russian until he noticed dark eyes staring at him. "Come," the woman said. "Join us."

The candlelight painted the family great-room with shades of dark coffee. The woman set out a plate of soft, fresh cheese and cut a sausage hard as wood into even slices. Wozniak banged down shot glasses and a bottle. He asked if the new Communist government was making progress in the towns.

"A long story!" Theo sighed. "Slavko sends regards." He untied the package, displaying two used boys' sweaters and fur-lined gloves. "Something for the body," he improvised, "something for the heart," and gently set down a small bottle of Cologne, "and something for the mind." He spread out some illustrated magazines.

The woman uncapped the bottle and sniffed, closing her eyes, while her husband clutched the stylish gloves in his calloused hands and sniffed. "Rabbit! Just the thing to shovel manure out of the stable. Well, Slavko must really need a favor!" He squinted in the hissing lantern light and picked up and read a magazine title aloud: "*The New Village*. A new Communist publication?"

"From Slavko's cooperative movement, for member farmers," Theo said. "But the boys will find some challenging word games."

The sons began flicking their fingers through *The Rural Household*. Wozniak pulled the lantern closer and donned his glasses. "Some useful articles on farm economics," Theo added.

"Farm economics?" Wozniak repeated. "If we give half our produce to our Polish landlords, what kind of farm economics can possibly improve our lot?" He leafed through the pages, while Theo studied his expression. "Well, I admit – impressive that my nephew can operate so openly right under the Poles' noses." He pointed to a column heading. "Can you believe this! MasloSoyuz is now exporting sour cream all the way to Belgium. The Belgians must really love it with their crepes!" He dropped the magazine and pulled the cork from the bottle. "So, the Poles let Slavko's cooperative take a few crumbs from their table. And now they're all crowing about it in Kalush like, like roosters." He poured out three drinks. Thanks.

I'll keep these magazines – At least our chicken coop could use some lining."

Theo ignored the prickly seed of anger forming in his throat. "Well, Uncle, Slavko had to negotiate some very rough political waters to keep the cooperatives operating."

"I'm sure he did," Wozniak said and stood up. "Those hills out there you've been admiring, where we used to collect firewood, pick berries –"

"And mushrooms," Wozniak's younger boy added.

"All off limits to us now!" Wozniak concluded. "Polish horsemen patrol it now." He broke a handful of kindling over his knee. "Polish settlers have been taking over this land for ten years—good land, Ukrainian land." He pushed the kindling into the stove and watched it catch fire. "And how? Simple! They claim our farms weren't legally registered. Imagine! Land passed down for generations – until one fine day!" He slammed the oven door shut. "And now we're waiting for the Communists to act – put an end to this Ukrainians groveling, this trying to appease our Polish landlords!"

"But why turn to Russians for help, Uncle?" Viktor said. "Join us and fight them together!"

Wozniak's eyes bored into him, "Join *us*? Who, exactly?"

Viktor's lowered his voice. "We can rebuild society together, but through Ukrainian power, not Russian power."

"Ah, Ukrainian power!" Wozniak snorted. "Some of you OUN boys stopped by last month, with your promises . . . your threats." He shook his head. "I asked what they'd do if they gained power; their plans … for farming credits, for education, for medical care." He laughed. "They hadn't even thought about it … whereas the Communists had!"

Theo wondered if Wozniak simply didn't know, or intentionally ignored the human devastation that Communist collective farms brought. But he held his tongue, until Viktor blurted out, "But the Holodomor—"

"Propaganda!" Wozniak overruled him. "No Socialist country starves a third of its own farmers to death! What was the Revolution for – if not for farmers and workers?" Theo exhaled slowly and looked away, as Wozniak's tone changed, his words harder, more deliberate." If we don't support the Communists and their iron fist, the Poles will one day fight back and restore their own order. And I know what that's like." He knocked back another shot glass, then limped to the back door and straightened up like a threadbare prophet. "Why do you think I limp like this? Some new fashion?"

"Why not put politics to sleep for a while?" his wife said.

Wozniak snatched a two-foot wooden flail from the wall. "Ever seen the Poles use one of these as a teaching tool?"

Viktor nodded. "I have!"

"Ever *felt* one?" Wozniak twirled the rod. "Boys, don't think your cooperatives"—and then glanced at Viktor — "or your slogans will protect us from this." His wife looked away as he smacked the rod against a log, dislodging a clump of bark. "And that's why we need an outside force with its own army. The Communists, and only the Communists, can break the Polish grip, and break it for good." He tossed down the flail. "I resisted the Poles and didn't sign a single one of their documents but paid the price. We held onto our land!" In the silence, the wind picked up, rattling against the windowpanes.

Theo saw only a blank, gray space where the icon corner once stood in the opposite corner of the room. Christianity must have deeply divided this marriage. He knew that their mission to find Viktor shelter here had failed, so why not end the diplomatic pretense, and leave with some dignity?

"I see you've studied Marx, Uncle," Theo quietly said. "May I pose a question before we leave?"

"Are you looking for instruction? I can summarize Communism for you," Wozniak interjected, limping back, "in two phrases: 'From each according to his ability'—"

"And 'to each according to his need,'" his wife mechanically completed her husband's sentence, and looked down.

"Beautiful words," Theo said. "But who decides what my ability is?"

"And who determines my needs?" Viktor added. "Not some Muscovite."

"Not at all," Wozniak said. "We will all work under one united economic plan and put aside our class differences. No fat landlords, no lowly peasants . . . no priests telling us to quietly accept our fates – like lambs!" He stood up and rewrapped the sweaters and gloves. "We'll be equal," he concluded. "And the *state* will ensure we're equal."

"A beautiful dream," Theo said. "The same beautiful dream that killed half of eastern Ukraine!"

"But a dream that's just as real as that pistol under your shirt," Wozniak quipped. "Your visit is over."

Theo stood. "Before we go, you should know—you should all know—in Kalush, the Russians are already purging local Ukrainian communists. Independent thinkers like—"

"Maybe they need to," Wozniak interrupted. "To rid the party of opportunists. Anyway, enough of this!"

Viktor stood up to leave.

"We can't just send them out into the night," Wozniak's wife said. "They're family! They said that they were in trouble."

Theo looked at his emaciated brother-in-law. "Viktor certainly is."

Wozniak stared at his wife. "Family," he said, "Those can be some of the most difficult. You know that yourself." He looked Viktor over. "Well, just how long does he need to stay?"

"In these times," Viktor said, "It's hard to say."

"Is someone looking for you?" Wozniak's wife asked.

Viktor sat back down and stiffened. The uncle continued. "Young man, are you escaping the draft?"

"No," Theo interjected. "Well, yes, just until this regime passes."

"So, our nationalist is a draft dodger too!" Wozniak concluded.

Viktor looked up and said, "I did a year in prison for my country—Polish prisons."

"Oh, we're all Ukrainians," the woman pleaded, her eyes shining, her sweater a pale pastel in the lamplight. "Doesn't out folk wisdom tell us, 'Who gives in need, gives doubly'? Take him in, at least for a few weeks."

Wozniak flipped the bottle back and forth between his hands. "Viktor's still young and stupid. And I kind of like both of you," he said. "All right, for the family's sake, he can stay for a week. But no longer!"

His wife began laying out blankets along ceramic ledges that extended from the fireplace out along the walls.

THE SOVIET ARMY, OR THE "RED ARMY," AS it was popularly known, was expanding at its fastest pace in its twenty-three-year-old history—unusual, given that the Soviet Union had just signed a nonaggression pact with Nazi Germany. In fact, the Red Army was secretly tripling in size, from 1.5 million in 1937 to a projected five million by 1941. Recruitment was proceeding quickly, with newly incorporated western Ukraine harnessed to supply more recruits under intense pressure to the goal of a fully mechanized, armored fighting force capable of continuing Communism's western expansion, an expansion temporarily halted at the Gates of Warsaw in 1920. And Stalin was not sparing his civilian population. A third of the Soviet economy was going into this attempt to produce the most modern war machine on the planet, while millions of underfed, poorly clothed Soviet workers lived and labored like serfs in the military factories.

German Intelligence, the *Abwehr*, knew of the buildup, but underrated the Soviet Union's ability to buy and adapt Western military technology, and the swiftness of the Red Army recruiting machine. Nor did the Abwehr notice Soviet metallurgical advances in tank armor meant to withstand direct anti-tank fire, nor new tank designs with retractable treads that gave way to tires meant to speed along Germany's Autobahns.

A horrific bloodletting of the Red Army officer corps also accompanied this rapid military expansion. In the coming clash with western Europe, Stalin had to assure himself of politically reliable officers. Extreme distrust characterized Stalin's psychology. As a tyrant with an ambitious schedule, he preferred quick amputation over precise surgery, and subjected almost the entire general grade officer corps to torture and execution, this bloodletting reaching down to the company level. Consequently, during this time of rapid expansion, the Red Army suffered an acute shortage of qualified officers. To fill the gap, politically reliable but often poorly trained men were promoted well beyond their qualifications.

AFTER THE CARRIAGE ROLLED INTO KALUSH, AN OBviously shaken Zosia described to Theo how the Red Army had forced their way into their house. It might have been on a neighbor's tip. Somehow, they had even found the trap door to the basement hidden under the kitchen rug. "They thought they'd finally found Viktor, Theo. Oh, thank God, Viktor left in time!" Zosia rewarded him with a kiss, and a bag of firm, red, freshly picked tomatoes.

But she said that the regime had begun arresting middle managers – though they were leaving Slavko alone for now. But she wondered why young adults had begun disappearing too – including those twins – just teenagers, who no one had seen for days. Theo thought of the lithe young woman with the limbs of a ballerina and refused to follow his thought any further. Just a coincidence – they'd turn up.

Zosia also cautioned him that the Red Army was starting to garrison officers in Ukrainian homes. But as she continued to speak, warning him, advising him, he found that her nearness, the lay of her hair, the generous Wozniak features and the overflowing feelings, made him long for Steffie again – at least for a temporary reprieve, until he could grapple again with the newest developments.

Once at home, he seized her immediately and slammed her back into the padded apartment door, then shut it, oblivious to the tomatoes spilling onto the floor. She pushed him back, wide-eyed, and stared to confirm his identity as his fingers entwined her waist.

She encircled his neck and gasped. "I take it the mission succeeded," she said, and pushed him back. "Theo, we have company." Theo heard the lilt of Russian, male voices. He turned and stepped quietly into the dining room, and stooped to retrieve an errant tomato. He saw two soldiers in green tunics at the table; one, with short, brush-like hair, standing and pointing a Nagant pistol. "And who might you be?" the soldier asked, slowly chewing.

"Just her husband," Theo said, trying to identify the man's rank from his shoulder boards. The soldier nodded to a tall man, perhaps a junior lieutenant, who leaped up and rustled through Theo's bag. Two Mosin rifles stood upright on the blue lacquered bench along the wall, their safeties not engaged, ready to fire, their bayonets reaching almost to the ceiling. With their short stocks, the ugliest rifles he'd ever seen, and with bruising recoils, he knew, but accurate as thunderbolts.

"Just tomatoes," the junior lieutenant quietly said, his moustache twitching.

"Good, we'll have them as *zakuski* (chasers), the higher-ranking soldier said, and turned to Steffie. "Go cut them up."

Theo unloaded the bag into the sink. "Lord, they eat like horses!" Steffie whispered, and slid the knife through the sharpener.

"And I see they found the booze," Theo whispered.

"That short one," Steffie said, and decapitated the first tomato, "gets lewd."

"And they're supposed to represent the Soviet Union's finest!" Theo said under his breath. He noticed a document on the kitchen counter entitled, "Certificate."

"The document says you gave them our clock voluntarily," Theo translated.

"I had to sign it."

The soldiers broke into "Stenka Razin," a Russian song new to western Ukrainians, about a warrior chieftain throwing his newly captured princess overboard, but only after an impromptu wedding and a night of debauchery, discarding her to preserve the crew's male unity. After a few bars, the junior lieutenant abruptly yelled for his *zakuski*.

Theo spotted the outlines of his father's clock wrapped in a pillowcase at the junior lieutenant's boots, and a row of civilian wristwatches adorning his wrist. He watched the lieutenant's fingers slide over Steffie's hand as she set down the plate. "So if he's your human being," he said to her, and pounded the table, "what does that make you? His goat?"

Theo knew the Ukrainian word for "husband" sounded like "human being" in Russian, another linguistic joke the occupiers reveled in, just as "to communicate" came out sounding like "to fornicate."

"No, no, you come sit over here, Mr. Human Being." The senior lieutenant turned to Theo and said, "I noticed all these books. An educated man. Misha, maybe we can learn something."

A drunken conversation followed, and ranged from the possibility of inhabitants on the dark side of the moon to the mystery of opposable thumbs. Was God or evolution responsible? At which point, the junior lieutenant broke in to introduce himself and his commanding officer, giving their names and patronymics, Russian-style, and proudly claimed the status of combat veterans of the recent war in Manchuria. The senior officer poured out another round and stood erect. "To comrade Stalin and the victorious Red Army!" Theo studied how their faces turned suddenly solemn at the name, Stalin. He had never heard of a war in Manchuria and wondered just how many rounds of vodka it merited.

"Why aren't you drinking with us, Mr. Human Being?" the junior Lieutenant asked.

"Maybe he resents being a new Soviet citizen," the senior Lieutenant said.

"You know, Mr. Human Being," the Junior Lieutenant said, "we have just three kinds of citizens in the Soviet Union. He suppressed a laugh. "– those in jail *now*, those that already *been* in jail," he pounded the table and howled, "and those that *will* be." He tried pouring himself another shot, but the senior officer lifted the bottle away.

"You're totally stupid – a goat!" the senior officer said, "And you're scaring our hosts."

The junior lieutenant picked up the Nagant and sullenly inspected both sides of the strange seven-chambered pistol. "Maybe he doesn't consider us his friends yet," he suggested.

"Could be another reason," the senior officer countered, and laid his hand on the pistol. "If you're so educated, why do you dress like a peasant?" he asked.

"He helps with the family farm on Saturdays," Steffie broke in.

The senior lieutenant turned back to Theo. "When did you last serve in the army?"

Theo felt his neck stiffen. "Army?" he repeated. "What makes you think—"

"The Red Army might need an educated man like him," the junior lieutenant added.

The senior officer held up his hand to quiet his companion. "You sure you never served?"

"No, I never served."

The senior lieutenant swirled the shot glass and stared at Theo. "But I think you served." He gulped down the vodka. "The way you looked at my rifle. A military look, like you're curious, not scared. You served in the Polish Army?"

"Me? I'm Ukrainian," Theo said.

"Ah, Ukrainian today," the senior lieutenant slurred, "Soviet to-morrow." He pointed the Nagant casually at a wall hanging of the Virgin Mary, stopped short of squeezing off a round, and pointed it back at Theo.

"Comrade Commander," the junior officer interrupted. "Maybe we could have us a Ukrainian song." He turned to Theo. "Can you play us something on that violin?"

"Of course he can play," the senior officer said. "All bourgeoisie play instruments." He staggered his way to the violin case.

Theo imagined another certificate to sign, another voluntary gift of his soulmate to his Soviet guests. "Actually," he said, "It's not a very good instrument. Defective!"

"Then maybe you don't need it," the senior officer concluded. He unsnapped the case and pulled out the violin, holding it by the neck like a bagged goose.

"Actually," Theo said, "my wife plays. Steffie please play us something."

Steffie stood, inhaled, and dragged the bow across the neck, releasing a series of unnerving screeches, until the lieutenant demanded she stop.

"You see," Theo said. "A defective instrument."

The senior lieutenant collapsed onto the couch, blinked a few times, and pointed at Theo and began snoring.

"Shouldn't you boys be getting back to the barracks?" Theo asked.

"We're here to stay until we get further orders."

OCTOBER 17, 1939

THE ANNEXATION

Moscow now owned half of Poland. The Communist Party began preparing eastern Galicia for annexation into the Soviet Union. The annexation had to appear legal to the watching world, and in strict imitation of the West's rule of law. Moscow had good reason to maintain its image as a liberator, not as an opportunistic conqueror, to keep themselves and the dozens of Communist movements throughout the world in a favorable light. According to Marxist doctrine, the workers of the world couldn't wait to join the happy family of Soviet nations. The first order of business: to indoctrinate the conquered population to vote in the right way in the coming election.

From October, workers throughout the annexed region had to assemble at lunch and after work, with armed soldiers to ensure participation. Opening speeches praised the Soviet Union and foretold a utopia, where airplanes would supply everyone's needs in quantities beyond imagination. Employees picked at random had to come forward to improvise speeches about these coming wonders. Anyone applauding with less than total enthusiasm appeared on a detention list. At the end of each rally, the crowds sang "The Internationale" and shouted, "Long live our dear Father Stalin!" Outside on the streets, schoolchildren carried banners proclaiming We Demand Stalin's Constitution.

At compulsory theater rallies, the regime marched out prominent eastern Ukrainians to describe the wondrous life in the Soviet Union, but as onlookers commented, they did so somehow without the joy that their words suggested. Local celebrities, often appearing pale on the stage, spoke positively of the world to come, some celebrities never to be heard from again.

Theo and Steffie followed the crowds to a theater rally one Sunday morning, with Joseph Stalin's portrait hanging center stage. As half a dozen Party men walked onto the stage and sat behind a green, felt-covered table, children in embroidered shirts ran to the stage and presented the speakers with flower bouquets. Theo recognized one of the panelists, Moskalenko—that same Moskalenko who had earlier posed as a Ukrainian patriot. Had he changed sides after the tanks rolled in? Or had he arrived as a Communist agent from the east? The two men knew each other by name and had spoken to each other freely.

By now, Theo knew that the NKVD had stationed observers in the back of the theater to identify anyone clapping without enthusiasm. Moskalenko rose to speak first in his soft Kyivan dialect. At the mention of Stalin's name, the panel shot up in mid-sentence and applauded. Theo and Steffie rose and clapped until Theo felt his palms turning numb. The auditorium thundered on for a full minute, five minutes, ten minutes until a cripple from the Great War finally collapsed into his chair, prompting the entire audience to drop to their seats, as if a trapdoor had sprung. At every mention of Stalin's name, the game repeated.

At the same time, the regime was compiling a slate of candidates for the general election. The party ordered each district to submit a list, but made it clear that it would only consider local candidates from the correct side of the Marxist class struggle, especially anyone with a history of breaking the law. Criminality demonstrated opposition to the bourgeois order. Proposing a bourgeois candidate from the UNDO, for example, subjected the proposer, and even the candidate, to arrest. In such cases, the party provided its own candidates from the Soviet Union. The elections committee then reduced acceptable candidates to one per district, giving voters one, and only one, choice.

On election day, so-called *Desiatniki* (Commanders of Ten)—themselves under threat of arrest for not fulfilling quotas—rounded up at least ten voters each. Whole streets then drove off in convoys under guard, as bands played patriotic songs. In some towns suspected of fervent nationalism, the NKVD took children as hostages to prevent unreliable parents from boycotting the election.

NKVD chiefs warned voters at the polling stations to vote "as the law says." Soldiers monitored the voting. In many towns, voters had to sign numbered ballots. Yet the regime insisted that such coercion was consistent with Lenin's principle of voluntary participation.

The elections concluded at the end of October. Ninety-three percent of voters elected fifteen hundred delegates, who assembled in L'viv four days later. The assembly voted to confiscate the remaining Polish estates and to nationalize the banks and successful enterprises, such as the dairy cooperative MasloSoyuz. The assembly then sent a delegation to Moscow to petition for formal inclusion into the Soviet Union. The one dissenting vote, a delegate from Chortkiv, Theo's home district, disappeared without a trace.

Three weeks later, the Supreme Soviet in Moscow formalized the annexation. Theo and Steffie were now living under a Soviet dictatorship.

AFTER THE ANNEXATION, KALUSH AWAITED SOME momentous announcement. The regime had chosen the school grounds for a big public assembly. The town began to gather as ordered.

What, if anything, would remain the same, Theo wondered? He looked for clues in yesterday's guest lecture in his art class. The Commissar for education had told his class the story of the schoolboy, Pavlik Morozov. Little Pavlik had violated the bonds of family loyalty, the lecturer had said, but for a higher cause. The boy had reported his own father to the town council for the crime of bartering for food. Even though it was during a food shortage and his family was hungry, Soviet authority still considered any kind of bartering "speculation," an economic crime against the Communist order. The council sentenced the father to death and awarded the boy a medal for his loyalty. The story could have ended there, the lecturer went on, but Pavlik's uncle took revenge on the little family traitor and split his head open with an ax. When the story reached Moscow, the regime declared the boy a Communist martyr and a hero for children to emulate. Statues of the Pavlik Morozov began to grace public squares.

Today Theo felt more like a lieutenant leading recruits on a forced march through town than a teacher of family values. He glanced back occasionally to guard against any frisky kicks or punches among his two dozen, white-collared schoolboys – especially Ivasyk, his class's number one mischief-maker that – truth be told – he secretly admired. Yet he couldn't imagine this tale of Pavlik Morozov influencing even Ivasyk, his most rebellious and unpredictable pupil. But who knew how certain children really regarded authority? Theo admitted to himself that sometimes he saw his own rebellious youth in Ivasyk and hoped that the boy's wildness would one day mature instead into something

... something even akin to genius. But he doubted Ivasyk would ever betray his father.

Theo continued leading his two dozen unruly pupils across the square and through the school's soccer field, and finally to a spot a soldier was pointing to, next to a class of teenaged girls monitored by nuns. Other soldiers were herding in streams of adults from the market. Female Soviet officers with some sort of—could it be?—yes, with alarm clocks suspended from their necks, were directing them into a makeshift enclosure, positioning the crowds to face the schoolyard. To his dismay, Theo, however, couldn't locate Steffie's kindergarten class anywhere in the crowds.

Ivasyk stepped out of line and limped toward him. Theo could see one knee bleeding down to his sock. The boy wanted to know if Mr. Teacher could excuse him to go to the infirmary. To his right, Theo saw militiamen milling under the eaves of the school building, smoking, coughing. He dodged eye contact. Better to avoid the school infirmary, he thought, as long as that bunch stood in the way.

Theo dropped to one knee, ready to dab the wound with a handkerchief, when a pair of NKVD squad cars parked next to the school. NKVD officers escorted a line of middle-aged men—underdressed for November, in shirts without coats—into the schoolyard. Of the five, Theo recognized the mayor, the police chief, and the railways superintendent, the town's VIPs. He expected to see Slavko, as director of MasloSoyuz. Instead, he saw the postmaster, and heard Ivasyk call out, "Tato!" The postmaster raised a hand and turned toward the boy, but the guard prodded the adult to keep walking. Ivasyk's father climbed the concrete stairs, and joined the other VIPs at the school wall. The militiamen under the eaves smoothed out each other's tunics and took turns adjusting the angles of their hats. Once they had it right, one of them uncorked a bottle and passed it around for one last pull. Fortified, the militiamen lurched into the courtyard.

The school's doors swung open. Theo recognized the school principal who joined the others. On command, the group turned toward the wall. The militiamen took quite some time fitting handcuffs onto the VIPs' back-turned hands. Again on command, the VIPs turned and faced the crowd. At that moment, a commotion erupted across the soccer field. The crowd parted to let some group come forward carrying aloft a professionally printed sign that stretched some five meters across, which Theo easily read from seventy meters away: "We demand class justice! Purge the social parasites!" Social parasites, indeed! Theo immediately thought of the real parasites, the so-called wild boars who took what they pleased. Theo was sure the sign couldn't be referring to them, but at this distance, Theo recognized no one in the mob across the grass, neither the men hoisting the sign, nor the gaunt woman stepping forward. She raised a bullhorn, the first he'd ever seen. The woman with an emaciated — or was it robotic?— expression asked the crowd how much longer workers had to suffer at the hands of their bourgeois exploiters. "The revolution is just beginning! Forget your fears, your inhibitions," she urged the citizens of Kalush, "and expose the parasites among you, as we exposed this group before you."

The mayor tried yelling over the bullhorn. The militiamen fitted a potato sack over his head, and over the heads of the other VIPs, the corners sticking up like double dunce caps. The militiamen took about ten steps back. The NKVD chief took the bullhorn from the woman and declared he had no choice but to obey the voice of the people. The citizens of Kalush should see how the state hears their pleas for social justice, and how it deals with class enemies.

Ivasyk bolted through the outer cordon. Theo hesitated. Yell for the boy to stop, or run to retrieve him? The NKVD chief raised his hand, as the boy turned and shielded his father's body. "Ivasyk!" the postmaster yelled. "Get out of here!" Surely, they would spare the boy, Theo thought. The chief dropped his hand.

Some of the first shots flew wide, ricocheting off the wall, but the enclosure kept the spectators from fleeing. The boy was among the first to fall. The postmaster dropped to his knees, and pitched forward onto his son. The mayor, his bag reddening, tried to crawl away. Theo turned from the second massacre he'd witnessed in two months. Several in the crowd fainted, as did the nun to his left. Had the Reds expected a carnival atmosphere, another French mob cheering the guillotines, instead of this dazed hush? The militiamen kept firing.

The scene repeated itself that day throughout western Ukrainian towns.

 COMMUNISM FELL INTO MORTAL CON-flict with conventional Christianity well before the Russian Revolution of 1917. Shortly after Karl Marx published *Das Kapital* in 1867, four successive popes recognized Communism as an implacable enemy to Christianity.

It wasn't so much Marx's call to overthrow civil authority and up-end all institutions, like the family, damnable enough in the church's eyes, but rather Marx's very denial of the spirit that so alarmed the church. Specifically, the church objected to a materialistic ideology that reduced human beings into cogs serving the state, a state that promised to satisfy all needs, but at the price of dictating all behavior, associations, and forms of expression; the epitome of a devil's bargain—earthly security at the price of the soul's freedom.

By contrast, the church promoted the cultivation of independent moral conscience as the path to salvation, a concept Communists dismissed as archaic nonsense. Morality answerable to God? An immortal soul? Eternal salvation? These notions stood squarely in the path of total state control. The individual didn't answer to some hypothetical God, he answered to the state! Communism was sworn to eliminate whatever stood between itself and its control of the individual, between itself and the paradise it promised in the here and now.

After the Communist Revolution overthrew the centuries-old Romanov dynasty in Russia, the patriarch of the Orthodox Church urged the faithful to resist the revolution's materialistic philosophy, even unto martyrdom. Stalin, who had once studied and rejected theology in his twenties, immediately responded to this defiance. Confident of an easy victory over organized religion, he authorized the People's Commissariat for Enlightenment to win over the citizenry through a series of public debates, fully expecting that backward Christian theology—mired, as he believed, in ignorance and medieval superstition—would simply wither when exposed to the light of progressive Marxist thought.

These highly anticipated debates sold out to standing-room-only crowds. But the judgement of the public went contrary to expectations. Orthodox clergy—well schooled in philosophical defenses against a string of heresies throughout church history—not only stood their ground against the Communist side, but made the more persuasive arguments, so much so that the organizers retreated, canceled the debates, and switched to straightforward "lectures on materialism." Yet so few voluntarily attended that Stalin lost patience and created a new agency to carry on the struggle, the League of the Militant Godless. The league launched a series of five-year plans to reinforce atheism.

Moscow began its war on religion by extending the ban on religious instruction from state to private schools—no teaching of Christian principles in *any* venue. Responding to widespread protests, the regime countered with a campaign of public ridicule, satirizing feast days and religious rites, with hooligans dressed as bishops and publicly burning sacred books. But such mockery failed to change minds. As if out of frustration, the regime then plundered the churches, chopped out the priceless ancient icons, and sold the country's religious heritage abroad. Moscow also officially designated the clergy agents of foreign terrorism, a capital crime under Soviet law. The five-year plans then degenerated into wholesale destruction and murder. As the 1930s ended, after the Great Purge had taken its toll, scarcely one in sixty churches remained standing in the USSR, and the Communist Revolution had executed in full two hundred thousand orthodox clergy, both Ukrainian and Russian.

After two decades of solid experience combatting religion, the Bolsheviks extended their atheistic struggle to western Ukraine, but with a new wrinkle. The NKVD had learned to allow a remnant of the church to keep operating, but under its own control, and to infiltrate the surviving clergy with its own trained agents.

A FEW YEARS EARLIER, BEFORE THE COMMUNIST movement forced its way into their lives, no one in the family anticipated Anton Wozniak's addiction. Even his wife considered his occasional card-playing harmless. But Theo's father-in-law, the principal of a Catholic girls' academy, began risking everything he had achieved in life.

As family patriarch, Anton Wozniak had been enjoying success—in family, in career, and in marriage. He had navigated Galicia's treacherous multi-ethnic politics to keep St. Basil's Academy funded and open. His wife, Maria, of the influential Korol family, had helped him build a coalition of Polish and Ukrainian politicians over dinner parties. Of his five children, four had survived into adulthood to show every sign of following in their parents' footsteps as leaders in the Ukrainian community. Every weekend, his family, all except for Steffie, turned loose their guitars, mandolins, and singing voices, Anton Wozniak's impromptu back-porch folk concerts attracting regular crowds.

The unravelling began after a dinner party. A Polish guest suggested the men try a few hands of Preference, a game that blended poker with bridge, at a local gambling den. The card dealers dressed like aristocrats. Expensive rugs and copies of Goya paintings completed the illusion of class. The imported cognac was on the house. The proprietors, veteran judges of character, recognized Wozniak as a mark. They played to his vulnerability, nodding to each other in fake admiration each time Wozniak met and raised the stakes. That first night, the worst thing that could have happened to Wozniak, happened. He won big!

He soon returned for more, and this time, alone.

He gradually dropped out of the weekly concerts. At Christmas, oddly, he failed to bring home the usual bonus. By mid-winter, Maria Wozniak noticed valuables disappearing from his study; the coat of arms, the bronze cast of a bandura player. Was he gambling? His answers seemed strangely illusive.

A month later, she found him taking out a loan from the *samopomich*, the community savings and loan. Finally, she confronted him. "Anton, do you have a gambling problem?"

With a dismissive wave of his hand, he admitted only to a "little financial problem," but really, nothing he couldn't handle. But her question seemed to sting him. He began taking solitary walks through the Carpathian foothills. Was he praying, seeking insight into his addiction? After a few restless weeks, the den welcomed him back, and assigned a young apprentice to cater to his whims. That night, a visitor, a friend from his first gambling escapade, saw a changed man, someone so obsessed behind the gambling table, that he took little note of him.

Wozniak had good reason to focus so intently. He was winning back the year's losses and much more, as the alarmed owners watched the headmaster's unusual streak. His friend stopped by the table, quietly urging him to quit and cash in his winnings. Wozniak instead doubled the stakes. His friend left.

When Anton returned well past midnight, he hesitated and stopped at Steffie's bed. He quietly sat, a bent figure. Steffie sat up and felt her father's frail body shaking with sobs. How could he face her mother?

Maria Wozniak had spent the night sleepless, trying to read, when she saw her husband enter the bedroom. "Don't hide anything from me," she insisted. He confessed he had lost—in fact, gambled away the family farm. They had let him keep the house, he quickly added, but he had lost that priceless multi-hectare property passed down through the Wozniaks for generations—gone! He reached for an embrace, but she stiffened. How did she know he wasn't scheming to win it back through another desperate loan? Or that he wouldn't gamble the house away, too? He shook his head and confessed to hitting rock bottom.

On Maria's insistence, Anton confessed to the parish priest, who agreed to enroll him in a private retreat, but only if he admitted he'd lost control of his habit.

Anton returned to his solitary hikes, trying to identify what was driving him to gamble. A vision changed his life. He came across a violently-writhing serpent in the road, on a clear, sunny afternoon. Anton later claimed to his skeptical wife that the unearthly creature calmed as he approached, and that it spoke to him, warned him with a voice he recognized. But whatever he'd actually seen had clearly shaken him to the core. His family saw him return to his faith with the enthusiasm of a new convert, even pausing to pray now at every roadside chapel they passed. He also purchased the largest and most true to life crucifix he could afford and installed his crucified Savior right in his office over his desk.

In the fall of 1939, Anton Wozniak had to face a new challenge: He wondered if the Communist takeover of western Ukraine voided the Concordat the Polish government had negotiated with the Vatican. Could he keep his Catholic school operating and still teach Christian morality?

 AFTER DEFEATING THE COUNTERREVO-
lutionary armies to win the Russian Civil War, the Reds
at once set to restructuring society. A top priority: replace religious instruction in the schools with Marxist
indoctrination. And for good reason: if the Revolution
was to succeed, the State needed not only an educated workforce but a
politically loyal one as well – to launch its vision of a completely new
and unprecedented Communist society.

Revolutionary dreams were one thing, but reality quite another.
The Reds found they had inherited a devastated education system.
Before the Revolution, over ninety percent of children had been attending school, but after years of war devastation and neglect, the figure had fallen to just a quarter.

Confronted with rampant illiteracy throughout the new Communist
realm, the new regime in Moscow found it had to temper its revolutionary zeal with common-sense practicality. To raise literacy levels quickly,
the government ordered basic instruction in all the local languages first -
including Ukrainian, Georgian, Belarusian, and the others. Russification
could come later. The Ukrainian language, suppressed for generations
under the Russian czars, enjoyed an unexpected rebirth, a surge in status and an outpouring of first-rate literature. The literary movement
reawakened a suppressed sense of national identity and, as it picked up
steam, took an independent turn, a turn that would aggravate Moscow.

Moscow made it clear that Socialist education was to serve the
needs of the State – and nothing else. No nationalist deviations, no
"knowledge for its own sake," no silly romantic poetry. School curric-
ula were to have only one aim: to produce graduates burning with the
vision of Communist's glorious future, graduates eager to implement
the Party's dictates.

When Joseph Stalin wrested power after Lenin's death, he added a
new twist. A doctrinaire Marxist in love with the notion of "struggle,"

Stalin introduced his own pet theory of evolution into education: As students struggled toward the glorious future that Marx had foretold, their struggle by itself eventually would yield a new kind of human being. The students, Stalin believed, would pass on their genes improved by struggle, generation by generation ... until the human being in Soviet society evolved into something special, something higher. Stalin called this advanced human life form "the New Soviet Man." Depictions of these futuristic hominoids began to appear everywhere – as statues, on posters, on postage stamps – their faces pulsing with Marxist fervor as they lunged toward the future – both genders in their prime and muscular as Olympic athletes. As a side benefit, the New Soviet Man would also be sexually liberated.

That very same year, newly appointed Reich Chancellor Adolf Hitler introduced a strikingly similar concept, the Aryan Superman, also a species of man that would evolve above the limits of mere biology – "Ein neues Lebensform," or "a new form of life," as Nazi propaganda proclaimed.

Ukraine, Russia's neighbor to the south, had concerns more down to earth than building new supermen, concerns much closer to home – like a just society with equitably distributed land, adequate educational opportunities, and a populace united by its common Ukrainian heritage and identity. Ukraine's Commissar for Education, Mykola Skrypnyk, a spitting image of a French Musketeer, saw the Revolution as nothing less than a historic opportunity to resurrect Ukraine to full autonomy. Ukrainian leaders began calling for economic and even political independence from Moscow. Every member country of the USSR, they claimed, enjoyed the right to construct its own path to Communism.

For Stalin, the Ukrainians of central Ukraine had gone too far. He saw their movement as nothing less than a counterrevolution. Echoing Lenin's dictum—"If we lose Ukraine, we lose our heads"—he and his inner circle concocted the most radical possible solution: full-scale genocide through controlled mass starvation– to bring the rebellious country to heel. In preparation, Stalin sent Pavel Postyshev to replace Mykola Skrypnyk, who saw his life's work discredited and, in an act of futile protest, committed suicide.

Stalin's eventual success in breaking Ukraine's drive for autonomy through mass murder expanded into the Great Purge, eliminating anyone at all who deviated or even appeared to deviate from his line. In 1939, the Purge was still raging throughout the Soviet Union when Stalin's regime occupied western Ukraine, and his commissars began visiting schools to ensure the strictest compliance.

THE TIGHTENING NOOSE

Anton Wozniak's first visitor that morning, a nun, curtsied. "Mr. Director, may I come straight to the point?" she said. "My girls need your protection."

"Protection? I take it this has to do with the commissar's visit yesterday."

The nun touched the crucifix resting against her black scapular. "This commissar—'commissar for education,' he calls himself—gave us a guest lecture, as we all had agreed," she said. "But he broached the topic of sexual morality with my class."

"Unusual," Wozniak said, "I thought Communists concerned themselves with economics."

"I did too," the nun said.

Wozniak leaned forward. "What business does he have to bring up such a topic?"

"He told them they were old enough to think for themselves. He offered to personally instruct them in, what he called, 'free love.'" The nun took a deep breath. "He asked for volunteers."

Mr. Wozniak gasped. "No! How old are your girls, sister? Fourteen? Fifteen?"

"No one knew what to say. Then one of the girls began to laugh, and then . . . and then the whole class started laughing."

"That old goat from Moscow might have thought that we're all just pushovers in some backward provinces," Mr. Wozniak said.

"He turned red and stood there like a stump. To save him further embarrassment, I suggested he might find what he's looking for at his own party headquarters."

"Well done, sister!" Mr. Wozniak exclaimed.

"I want to protect my girls from any repercussions," the nun concluded, as Wozniak scribbled on a block note. "Will you be attending the patriarch's conference today?" she asked.

The door swung open. The nun rose, and stared at the intruder, a man in his thirties in a blue-trimmed visor cap. Wozniak motioned to the nun to see if this was yesterday's guest lecturer. The commissar cut her off, and demanded that she leave the room.

"Mr. Director," the nun said, "you have my prayers."

The commissar studied the office's layout and paused to stare up at the crucifix. He tossed his blue cap onto the principal's desk, revealing curly hair encircling a premature bald spot. He tilted his head to examine the titles in the bookcase, and began pulling out books, letting them drop onto the floor.

"Is this the civilized behavior we can expect now from Moscow?" Wozniak said. "Please pick up each one of those books."

The commissar pulled out a large folio from a middle shelf, and leafed through until he found a document that seemed to interest him. Silently moving his lips to form the Ukrainian words, he said, "You keep good meeting records." He dropped the folio onto the discarded pile and adjusted the angle of the guest's chair, sat, and crossed his legs. "You need to get your staff under control," he said, his accent heavy, his gray eyes magnified behind the strong lenses. He extended a cigarette case toward the principal. "Smoke?"

Wozniak ignored the gesture and began replacing the books. "I cannot approve smoking in a religious school." He paused. "Or visitors disrupting my classes."

"And we can't approve you teaching young citizens any more religious nonsense," the commissar said. He blew a lungful of smoke at the erect principal and motioned for him to sit.

Wozniak shook his head. "My dear sir," he said, "according to the 1924 concordat between the Vatican and Poland, as a private religious school, we—"

"Poland?" The commissar chuckled. "There is no more Poland."

"According to the concordat," Wozniak repeated, "our school answers to Rome." He checked his wristwatch and added, "I will have to ask you to leave. I have a meeting."

"Cancel it," the commissar said.

"Cancel it?" Wozniak repeated.

"Cancel it!" the commissar said, and pulled out his revolver. "You can begin by taking down that crucifix."

"The crucifix?" Wozniak stalled. "Only the custodian can do that," he said.

"So, send for him!"

The custodian hesitated at the sight of the blue NKVD hat on the desk. He said that only the superintendent of schools could authorize such an action.

The commissar dropped his cigarette onto the waxed floor and crushed it under his boot, holstered his pistol, and shoved the desk against the wall, then the chair against the desk.

"Wait, comrade commissar," Wozniak pleaded. "I propose a compromise." The commissar paused and squinted. "We can easily put up Soviet portraits on either side of the crucifix; Stalin on one side, Lenin on the other." Then he added a sentence that he would regret for what remained of his life: "Like the two thieves on either side of Christ."

"A comedian!" The commissar hissed and hopped onto the desk. He slammed down the meter-long crucifix, fracturing the torso, and the head rolled to a stop at the custodian's feet. The commissar jumped to the floor, one boot landing on the broken crossbeam. "Without permission to occupy this building, Citizen Wozniak," he said, wincing, "you are trespassing on state property." He hobbled off.

The custodian laid out the broken crucifix on the principal's desk and tried to fit a severed arm back to the torso. Wozniak looked out the window at the commissar limping toward a waiting sedan. "I certainly earned a place of honor in his files," he said.

"Mr. Director," the custodian whispered. "None of my business, but do you think we're strong enough to stand up against a regime like that? Why antagonize the man any further, Mr. Director? You know, the Russian Czar once tried to drive the Order of Saint Basil out of Ukraine – and nearly succeeded. Maybe – maybe you should reconsider attending that meeting."

"No, Mr. Yuriy, no!" Mr. Wozniak said and sighed. "This commissar is seriously overplaying his hand." He paused and added, "He's bluffing."

THE NEW REGIME'S SMILE OF GOODWILL faded. By November, the secret police had eliminated western Ukraine's cultural and political institutions, and set about fulfilling Moscow's arrest quotas for the new province.

To purify society, the Soviets routinely began by designating an initial 10 percent of the population as "enemies of the people"—nationalists, the clergy, military officers, attorneys, entrepreneurs.

If arresting such categories of enemies fell short of the 10 percent quota, the regime widened the dragnet to include citizens with relatives overseas, anyone getting foreign mail, and even Esperanto enthusiasts. If the resulting arrest statistics still fell short, the secret police simply took to arresting local people at random, claiming to have uncovered spy rings and then forcing the required confessions.

The new regime had promised to improve the town's infrastructure, but Theo interpreted the new wave of hasty concrete-block construction as nothing more than a sign of more arrests to come. The construction included several new NKVD interrogation centers too – one directly across the lane from his apartment.

To prepare for the anticipated case load in western Ukraine, Soviet secret police chief Lavrentiy Beria had lowered maximum investigation time from thirty days for a case to just ten days. This abbreviated period put unprecedented pressure on the interrogator to extract confessions, since interrogators themselves became subject to arrest for not meeting quotas. These pressures opened the public to random arrests on a mass scale.

Finally, the local population did not suspect that the NKVD was introducing a new mass interrogation system credited to a certain Sergeant Yurii Pospelov. Pospelov had improved on a popular Soviet technique borrowed from the Middle Ages, called the yoke. Two investigators normally worked over a single prisoner for a full day, curling the body backward and bending the feet to the head; in the process, stretching and snapping vertebra. The yoke left permanent internal damage but no visible marks. Pospelov cleverly converted the yoke into an assembly line process, whereby just one interrogator could efficiently torment an entire basement full of prisoners.

Stalin knew that Western courts dismissed confessions extracted by force. He ordered the NKVD to carefully document interrogation sessions, but in such a way as to exonerate its interrogators from

wrongdoing. It wasn't the fault of the interrogator if the prisoner refused to cooperate. The prisoner was at fault. Comrade Pospelov himself complained of the burdensome paperwork he had to fill out in ink
whenever a prisoner failed to survive one of his interrogation sessions.

FOR GENERATIONS NOW, UKRAINIAN CATHOLIC
priests went beyond meekly preaching and administering the
Sacraments. In the countryside, they worked hard with their hands and
mixed with countryfolk. The faint-hearted need not apply – because
the Church in western Ukraine spread not only the Gospel, but basic
literacy and rural development. The priests hung up their vestments
after Mass, and rode out on horseback on Monday morning to demon-
strate new farming practices, and to urge their tradition-bound and
often suspicious congregations how to organize themselves into cooperatives, and then market their surpluses – clear challenges in remote
mountain villages steeped for centuries in pagan lore and superstition.
The Church got a boost in her mission when Austria took over western Ukraine from Poland. The Austrian Kaiser applauded the Church's
work in eastern Galicia, the Reich's poorest new province, and set up
Western Ukraine's first formal seminaries – to reinforce the priest-
hood's dual duties – to render both unto God and unto the Kaiser.

But the Austrian Empire itself fell after the first World War, and
western Ukraine went back to Poland. For the time being, the Poles
tolerated these Ukrainian seminaries, but categorically prohibited
Ukrainian universities. With Ukrainians excluded from higher education, a seminary education remained one of the few options left to
ambitious young Ukrainians – whether they felt a religious calling or
not. At the seminary, they could at least learn rhetoric and logic, pick
up church history, study great Eastern Tradition theologians like St.

Basil, and even learn some rural economics. With time, the rectories grew wary of this flood of new impostors feigning piety.

And Steffie's brother Vlodko clearly did not fit the mold of a traditional, pious Catholic seminarian. Though he studied hard, his bawdy sense of humor had raised the eyebrows of his fellow seminarians. Steffie, for one, saw more of an assertive ladies' man than a devout cleric in Vlodko. His brother Slavko agreed. He admired Vlodko's prowess in the boxing ring, but not at all his approach to interpersonal problems. Vlodko had used bare knuckles more than once when crossed. Vlodko's father had assumed all along that his son had enrolled for the education, and would, like so many other Ukrainians – like Theo, in fact – simply drop out when asked him to take the life-changing vows of poverty and obedience to the Church.

To his family's disbelief, this blunt alpha male, Vlodko Wozniak, accepted Holy Orders.

The Ukrainian Catholic hierarchy prudently assigned its new, plain-speaking graduate to three isolated Carpathian villages right among the Hutzuls, a remote and superstitious people with shamans practicing magical rituals. Vlodko dutifully obeyed. As the Communist regime started transforming western Ukraine and as the new regimes' tax burden on churches began rising, the alarmed Hutzuls began filling Vlodko's church to capacity. The revolution began to penetrate the remote mountains.

Shrouded now in a cloud of incense and choral singing, Vlodko raised his hand to bless the congregation in preparation for the day's Gospel reading, and then turned back toward the wide iconostasis with its solemn Byzantine saints – the holy sextet solicitously gazing down on him, the newly ordained parish priest. Knowing that Byzantine rite priests can marry, the parish's younger women, in embroidered, contoured Hutzul jackets – cheeks rosy from the cold, heads covered in bright red scarves, had gathered toward the front of the church

– seemingly for a closer glimpse at the eligible new bachelor saying Mass. And indeed, the flowing vestments couldn't disguise Father Vlodko Wozniak's athletic build. And the slant of the late autumn sun sharply emphasized his square, dimpled jaw, his high forehead, and thickset nose – a muscular caricature of the Wozniak family's Byzantine-icon appearance.

Vlodko turned back toward the congregation and critically viewed his two altar boys clutching gold-trimmed candles. He loudly berated them – that's now where he wanted them to stand – instead, they should position themselves just two feet from the lectern. As the boys adjusted, a third altar boy ran in from the sacristy, pointed to the doors, and whispered. The priest opened the silver-framed book to the page marked with a red ribbon and motioned the boy back to the sacristy. He looked past the shaggy-haired Hutzul men in the rear standing upright in their heavy sheep-skin coats, and saw the double doors still closed behind them.

He began orating the day's reading to celebrate the Feast of the Immaculate Conception, which this year fell on a Friday – when suddenly light burst in, overexposing the candle-lit interior.

Against the open doors, the silhouette of a commissar in a field cap strode into the nave, with a taller uniformed man in lockstep behind, their boots clicking together. To either side, parishioners were holding aloft religious banners, with one Hutzul clasping the image of Mary and her infant depicted in a silver monstrance, with silver spokes radiating outward like burning phosphorus. The two intruders marched to the center, scrutinizing the glittering walls and gazed up at the mosaic-studded cupola.

"Why is this church full on a weekday?" the commissar demanded.

"What business is that of yours?" Vlodko responded in his bass voice. "If you haven't come here to pray, get out!"

"Tell your congregation to clear the church immediately," the uniformed man said.

"Do you think you're in a tavern?" Vlodko said, "Have you cleared your visit with the metropolitan. If not, you are trespassing."

The commissar stepped forward. "Not so," he said. "It's you, priest, who are trespassing. You are illegally occupying state property."

"Appropriated for non-payment of taxes," the sergeant added.

"A totally false claim," Vlodko said, and raised his hand to calm the congregation. "This church still answers to Rome."

"This church answers to Moscow," the commissar replied, "And Moscow doesn't peddle your hocus-pocus."

"And what kind of hocus-pocus does your Moscow peddle?" Vlodko shot back.

The commissar strolled to a wood-panel painting, an image of St. George thrusting a lance through a dragon's throat. He reached behind the painting, felt for something, straightened up, and said, "Good! Start with this one. Call them in."

A squad of soldiers in gray winter coats and peaked hats filed in carrying saws and crowbars as the hushed congregation gave way. Two soldiers grabbed the icon's silver-encrusted rims, yanked, and began carrying the icon out.

"Soldiers! Clear it all out—anything you can hammer or saw off," the sergeant ordered "Do not damage any of it."

"Stop!" Vlodko commanded. "In God's name, stop in your tracks!" The sergeant froze in mid-step and turned back, his eyes darting back and forth between his superior and the priest.

As Vlodko approached, the commissar's hand dropped to search for a non-existent holster. "What's this?" he chuckled, "A priest not turning the other cheek?" Vlodko grabbed him by the right arm, but when the commissar tried to throw a punch with his left, the priest blocked it, ready to drop him, if need be, with a clear, unimpeded right cross to the jaw.

 BOTH US PRESIDENTS WOODROW WILSON and his successor, Herbert Hoover, refused to recognize the Soviet regime, which they considered a criminal enterprise. Instead, Hoover sent diplomats to the neighboring Baltic countries as monitors. Back in Washington, these diplomats created the US State Department's first eastern European section and organized a library to chronicle the Soviet regime's deeds.

In 1933, at the time of the Great Famine in Ukraine, the new US president, Franklin D. Roosevelt, broke with his predecessors and formally recognized the Soviet regime—and found an ambassador to send to Moscow, fully sympathetic to Stalin. After attending a series of show trials of alleged anti-Soviet "wreckers," the new ambassador favorably compared the Soviet legal system with that of the United States.

Despite Franklin D. Roosevelt's warming to the Communist state, the State Department's eastern European section held on to its own opposing views. Annoyed, Stalin pressured the American president to disband the section. In 1937, Roosevelt ordered the staff reassigned, and their library crated up and shipped away to the Navy Yard. An approving Stalin then dispatched his chief spymaster in 1938 to assassinate the leading Ukrainian political émigré in Holland.

"HE KNOCKED THE COMMISSAR OUT, ACTUALLY floored him in front of the congregation!" Theo repeated.

"You don't know my brother," Steffie said and set down two bowls between them. "Afterward, the parishioners had to hide him. Of course, he didn't think of that."

"And the church?" Theo asked.

"Shut down."

Theo knew the cabbage soup would taste stringy, cold. Last week his neighbors had already broken off the last of the tree limbs in the lot across the street for fuelwood and were now starting on the fences.

"He may have even broken the commissar's jaw," Steffie said.

Theo wondered if eastern Ukraine could have stopped the terror-famine and thrown the Russians out – if his countrymen had acted like Vlodko and all risen together. That was the key – if they had all risen together. "I can't help but admire him," he added.

"You do?"

"Someone's got to stand up to them."

"Stand up to them? That's what you said? Didn't we watch the NKVD surround the Prosvita building on Monday and haul away our friends, our best friends? Didn't you hear the accordions again last night?"

Of course, he had I heard them. He knew full well that the NKVD had taken to live accordion music to try to masquerade their interrogation sessions.

"What if one night we recognize the voice of someone we know?" she pressed on.

Last night he'd awoken to Steffie hiding her head under the pillow. He'd heard it all, too, but had somehow blocked it out—as none of his business. Maybe, he thought, maybe after the NKVD had eliminated the leadership, like they had done at the soccer field they would rest ... for a while.

He watched her inspecting the walls now, as if searching for some structural weakness. "After a while, it hardly sounds human," she said. He reached across to her, his fingers sliding to the fragile collarbones underneath the sweater. He was about to say that he believed the worst was probably over.

A knock on the door made Steffie stare at her husband. "It's too late for the mailman," she said.

"If it's that neighbor," Theo said, "tell her we've run out of flour too."

A second louder knock led to Steffie rattling the chain and locking it into place, then opening the door a crack. Theo heard whispering back and forth, and she turned back to him. "He's asking for you, Theo."

He recognized the familiar eyeglasses—Moskalenko, the mole, the collaborator, in civilian clothes again. Theo studied those intense eyes that had seemed so reassuring just two months ago. Those same eyes stared back just as intently. "Listen carefully," Moskalenko whispered. "I reviewed the arrest lists. They're coming for you in three days, Mr. Diachok—three days." Moskalenko looked around and added, "Don't tell anyone I came here!" He walked off into the semi-dark corridor, looking down as if checking something on a clipboard.

Theo closed the door and backed away, blinking, staring at the lock. "It's just a mistake. Someone must have mixed up names," he said. "Or . . . some kind of disinformation."

"We both heard him," she insisted, staring at him. "Theo, where are you going?"

Theo walked into the bedroom and locked the door. Outside the window, the wind was swirling the snow into tufts that slowly drifted away like colonies of forgotten, lost souls. He opened the violin case, picked up the bow, and balanced it in his fingers. It was, of course, time to practice Schubert.

He heard Steffie's hand rattling the door handle as she said, "Didn't you understand, Theo? They're coming for you."

2ᴺᴰ REALITY CHECK

I found my father sitting on the edge of the bed, his head bowed and resting on his hands that clutched his walking stick. He lifted his head as I walked in. I sat next to him, close enough to breathe in his scent; the scent that had always meant that nothing could hurt me—not as long as he was here.

"What kind of a life is this, son?" he said to me. "How can I go on?"

He told me he just shuffled with his geriatric cane from the make-shift bedroom out to the kitchenette and back, not quite ten meters—not even enough for a first down in American football. With his congested heart, he was in danger of forfeiting today's contest. He'd fallen behind and his eyes pleaded with me.

"Tato, do what you've always done: Keep your boots on and face the direction of the battle," I said.

My father's gaze softened. He nodded, half smiled. Maybe he understood that I wanted—needed—to see courage in him. His face flickered with gratitude; gratitude for reminding him of his duty. Someone appreciated the life path he'd chosen long ago, and the whole nine yards left to him.

"I admire you for going on with that book," he said. "But you might be wasting your time. Few people may be willing to read something so"—he searched for a phrase—"so at odds with what they know from Hollywood movies."

My sister interrupted, wordlessly setting down a tray of chamomile tea and Canadian winter-wheat biscuits on the night table. My father's eyes lit up at his only daughter, who'd inherited his Nordic features, his musical gifts. She folded the doors shut again with a noiseless, self-effacing style she shared with him. His fingers withdrew from the still-hot tea pot.

"In November—a brutally cold November," he began, "Soviet trucks started hauling cement, some massive building campaign. I could see by the crude construction that it wasn't schools; no, more prisons, because they were already overfilled. Soon, practically every family we knew was in tears; they'd arrested someone's father, or son, or uncle. Sometimes when I walked by, I could hear them yelling together for water.

"In the morning, you could see lines of women and children standing in the frost, waiting for news. Was a husband or a son still in prison? Or had he been transferred? They'd all brought something for the prisoners; a pot of soup already turned cold, some vegetables wrapped up in a newspaper. Could the guard pass it on? Sometimes I'd see the arrested men led out for transfer—some with broken, discolored hands, one, even an empty eye socket—the guards shoving them all to move faster. I once saw a woman, maybe someone's wife, walking back. She collapsed to her knees on the sidewalk and let out a little cry of despair, then picked herself up and went on.

"At that time, the Soviets introduced a system of anonymous denunciations. Posters appeared encouraging us to report our neighbor for "anti-Soviet" attitudes. And the NKVD always seemed to come for them at two in the morning. A lot of people took to leaving town at night to sleep in the countryside, and then come back for work in the morning."

My father fell silent. I noticed the afternoon sunlight playing on his forehead. As he approached ninety, his eyebrow ridges stood out now, almost like two sand bars at the beach. My mother, an amateur phrenologist, had once called those ridges his twin peaks of mathematics and music. The basin between those ridges, and his still-full hairline, had also deepened. His good looks, trim proportions, aquiline nose, had all survived, despite the thin, leathery skin that sometimes looked transparent. In just a month, on Montgomery General Hospital's third floor, I'd run my hand over and over across that forehead, and it would feel increasingly like cold rawhide.

He looked at me as if to say, "Life—we can't do anything to change it." He continued. "You know, we Slavs somehow see life in a spiritual way. You can hear it in our music, our poetry. But at times—at times, I just can't believe in God. The best people were always the first to go; the best teachers, the best people at Prosvita, our writers, our composers." He looked at me as if half expecting an answer. "Why was I spared?" he asked.

I closed my spiral-bound notebook. In the silence, we could hear the TV cheerily announce from the family room next door that Slobodan Milosevich would have to stand trial for ethnic cleansing in former Yugoslavia.

"Ah . . . war crimes," my father said, exhaustion having drained his face into a buttermilk-like pallor.

THE ESCAPE ATTEMPT

When Steffie walked in, she noticed the closet door ajar and sniffed the air. "You're not developing pictures again?" she called out, and threw her coat onto the chair.

Theo stepped out and shut the door to the bedroom closet he'd converted into a darkroom. "The red light went out again!" he said. "I wasted a quarter of a liter of—"

"Theo," she said, reaching for his shoulder. "You've got two days left. You won't find a solution in the dark room."

He pivoted to avoid her touch. "Solution?" he said. "Solution to what?" He picked up a magazine, scanned the cover, and tossed it back onto the table. "They've got my name, and they'll just keep arresting us until they get their quotas." He turned toward her. "And where were you?"

"Trying to find someone who can help us." She lowered her voice and said, "There may be a way out. Slavko said that the Russians are letting ethnic Germans transfer out of here to the German zone. Do you understand? All we need is a set of German passports."

He laughed. "Oh, is that all we need?" He rambled back and forth through the room like a bear testing a cage. "Why do you believe fairy tales like that, Steffie? By now, the Russians have gotten their paws on my records, just as the Germans will." He stopped pacing and looked down. "I realized something, Steffie. If I don't go and face my arrest like a man, they'll just take someone else. Would that be fair? To have someone else take my place? It's just my turn."

"Do you know what you're saying?" Steffie asked.

"And if somehow I do escape," Theo interjected, his eyes refusing to meet hers. "Then what? They'll arrest my family in Hadynkivtsi – as revenge, as a lesson. You see, I really have no choice."

"No one they've arrested—"

"I know," Theo said irritably, "No one's –"

"No one's returned. And you won't," she said. "You know, don't you, that they found the bodies of that missing teenaged boy and his sister. – both mutilated." She dropped to one knee and reached for his chin and turned his head until their eyes met. "Moskalenko tipped you off because he sees something in you worthy of risking his life," she said. He examined her dark eyes. She drew his hands toward her until his fingertips touched her belly, and whispered, "Did you know that at nine weeks, a baby already has fully formed fingers?"

"You're not expecting?"

She searched his eyes. "You know that if they execute you as an enemy of the people, they'll send me, carrying our child, to Siberia."

Theo felt as if a finger had released a long-clogged valve in his heart.

They began with Viktor's old contacts in the OUN, and then worked their way deep into the black market until well past curfew. That night, they located someone promising, an enterprising some- one who offered them a stack of passports to review; passports from dead German settlers that Poles had massacred during the September invasion. But only one passport, from the dozen they examined, seemed to fit their profile; from a young deceased German couple, Wilhelm and Anna Stemmler. The problem was that such passports reflected Germany's strict Protestantism—until death do us part—with photos of husband and wife mounted together on the same page. Though Theo and the deceased German looked nearly alike—practically twins—Steffie, a slender brunette, in no way resembled Anna Stemmler, a chunky blonde. When Theo wavered, Steffie insisted they exchange their carton of cigarettes at once for the leather-bound passport. They would just have to find a way, and had little time before the next morning's opening session at refugee control.

In the dark of early morning, Theo reached into his store of theatrical makeup to try to transform his bride somehow into a prosperous German hausfrau. Peach-colored makeup, heavily applied, might make her look fleshier. A blonde wig and a green mountaineering hat, though long out of vogue, would complete the job. "This is so poorly thought through!" Theo mumbled, while he worked the makeup.

"Keep going, Theo. You're very talented."

But when he finished, he saw not Steffie, but a big doll, like a giant Christmas gift for a German child.

At eight in the morning, they presented their passport and a signed affidavit claiming German heritage at the new center to control population movements. They'd have to pass Russian and then German control points. And they'd have to wait their turn in the crowded hallway with other couples and solitary applicants, who seemed to stare at every new newcomer as if on guard against anyone faking their way through. And they waited. At least the building was well heated, and beads of perspiration began forming on Steffie's thickly made-up forehead. She sat stiffly, not daring to remove her extra-heavy coat, meant to plump out her contours. "Try to relax," Theo whispered. "You're beginning to attract—"

"I *am* totally relaxed," she hissed.

The Russian emigration office door burst open. Theo caught a glimpse of three inspectors behind a green felt table. "Sure, sure, you're as much a German as I am," an immigration officer mocked.

Two men, pistols drawn, hustled a woman past him. The officer's assistant called out for the next interview. As a couple stepped in, the assistant shut the door.

"Steffie!" a woman's voice called out. "Is that you, Steffie?"

Theo turned around. "Who is she?" he whispered.

Steffie whispered, "A friend from teacher's college."

The young woman in her fashionable feathered hat stooped to peer closer – to Theo, like some inquisitive mother hen. "Steffie, what's wrong? And why that strange wig?" Theo saw other couples looking up. Steffie glared back, fingers to her lips.

By noon, the makeup began to run freely. When the assistant announced the next applicant, they both sat motionless. The name Stemmler hadn't yet registered in Theo's mind. "No Stemmlers here?"

"Yes, that's us!" Theo called out, and quickly ran his palms across the smeared makeup in a final attempt to Germanize his wife.

A high-cheek-boned officer in his mid-thirties was examining an application on his desk, next to a crank-up military telephone nestled between teacups and passports. Red rectangular patches with gold trim adorned the officer's collars. "So you're also Germans," the officer said casually. "We'll see." His two assistants looked up lazily at the couple. Theo recognized the shorter assistant reaching for the teapot—yes, the very same fellow who'd promised Theo "You'll sing for us," when the Red Army first rolled in. "And here . . . is your passport," the control officer said, Theo detecting the unmistakable Moscow accent, the lengthened a's, as in "pays-port." The officer looked up at Theo with the gaze of a trained interrogator, the trusting eyes meant to disarm you into divulging your secrets. He squinted and nodded, and asked Steffie to raise her head, and then, a smile playing on his face, motioned for her to straighten up completely.

Was he blind to the streaks, or did he admire the couple's audacity? Did he feel guilty about sending the last impostor to her death? "With papers like these," he drawled, "we'll just have to shoot you." He smiled and reached for the "approved" stamp. His two listless NKVD colleagues looked up from their tea and waved the couple through. Theo and Steffie stumbled over each other exiting the office, Theo fighting to regain composure to negotiate the next minefield.

When the soldier ushered the couple into the main welfare office for ethnic Germans and smartly clicked the door behind them, Theo felt he'd entered a parallel universe. In contrast to the Russian bureaucrat's regulation green outfit, the German consul looked like a university rector in his tailored gray suit. A photograph of a young, wistful Adolph Hitler hung above his desk. Those eyes, Theo thought, penetrating, intelligent, but nearly liquid with some sort of victimhood! Theo knew little about Hitler, except that he'd built futuristic superhighways, and had put Germany's unemployed back to work. Oh, yes, and last year, an American magazine had named Hitler "man of the year."

The consul, well into middle age, limped out from behind his desk to shake hands. Seeing the man's labored shuffle, Theo stepped toward him, but was waved away. "Wounded on the Russian Front. The Great War, 1918," the consul said with a Bavarian accent. "So! The Reich welcomes back her children! But we must be sure of you." Then he added, "Cigarette?"

The man's geniality reminded Theo of the cheerful German troops who'd occupied his father's house a generation ago.

"Mrs. Stemmler, what language do you speak at home?"

"Naturally, we mix German and Ukrainian," Theo interjected. "Living abroad, our vocabulary is naturally more developed in the local language."

"Naturally. Who is your favorite German poet, Herr Stemmler?"

"Without question, Goethe."

"And your favorite work by Goethe?"

"*Faustus*. Incomparable!"

"Incomparable? Didn't you find it a little pretentious? I've always preferred his *Trilogy of Passion*. Know it? No? Mrs. Stemmler, I haven't seen an alpine hat like that since the film *The Mountain Calls*. Where did you pick it up?"

Steffie threw a panicked glance at her husband and bowed her head.

The official repeated, "Where did you find such a hat, Mrs. Stemmler? Mrs. Stemmler, do you speak German? *Are* you German?"

The consul struggled to his feet again to approach Steffie. Theo embraced her, whispered to her, and said, "Esteemed Mr. Consul, my wife is nauseated. In her second month of pregnancy. She may . . . need to vomit."

"Ich . . . krank" (I . . . sick), Steffie croaked in German, to some prompting.

"Ah! In that case—in that case, why keep you any longer?" the consul said, eyeing his Persian rug.

They walked out of the main welfare office with freshly typed transfer permits, train tickets, and ration cards—with extra rations for Mrs. Stemmler's pregnancy, presumably because the Reich needed healthy boys for the new future beginning to unfold.

They collapsed onto a snow-covered bench facing the white crenulated towers of St. Valentine's Catholic Church. Behind them, workers were pouring the foundations for a new prison. Sweet, crisp air had followed in the wake of the snows. Column after column of storks, reflecting the sun like shards of glass in the ice-blue sky, sliced their way toward Africa. Theo's legs began shaking first, then Steffie's. It was a full five minutes before their nerves settled. They agreed not to return home. The resident collaborator would likely inform the NKVD of anyone leaving with packed suitcases. They'd have to rely instead on the valuables they had crammed into their coat pockets; that, and their new ration cards.

They escaped arrest by eight hours.

ON THE DAY THAT THEO AND STEFFIE SUC-cessfully navigated the population checkpoints, the League of Nations took a momentous step, having finally lost patience with Soviet behavior. The League, a precur-sor to the United Nations, had witnessed Communist Russia terrorize the small Baltic States of Lithuania, Latvia, and Estonia into accepting military bases. The League then helplessly watched Stalin annex a third of eastern Europe, under the most transparent pretexts.

Stalin then followed through on the nonaggression pact's secret protocol, and invaded Finland with a mechanized million-man army. In this case, Stalin's foreign minister presented the pretext that the Soviet Union was protecting itself from its tiny "fascist-aggressor" neighbor. The League finally expelled the Soviet Union from the com-munity of nations.

The list of expelled, rogue nations had just expanded, and Russia found herself in the strange company of Italy, Japan, and Germany. Adolf Hitler, distrustful of Western intentions, had forced Germany to quit the League when he took power. Central Europe, all the way to the Ural Mountains and beyond, now fell into a rogue zone, where international law no longer applied.

THE CLOSED VOWELS OF THE RUSSIAN LANGUAGE, grating to the Ukrainian ear, echoed from loudspeakers at the train station. Theo peered into the long cylindrical space along platform one, a space that dissolved into nothing but darkness. He turned from the empty tracks to the anxious faces around him, trying to distinguish genuine ethnic Germans from fellow imposters. He thought he spotted a few. A squad of Russian soldiers lined up on the platform across from them. He felt Steffie press against him. "Perhaps," she said, "perhaps you go on without me. Really, how can I just abandon my family at a time like this?"

"Steffie, they will have to take care of themselves," Theo whispered. "You've never been away from your family, have you?" Loudspeakers crackled to life again. "So strange to hear German here," he added, and took her arm. "Come, a change of track."

"Theo, I should go back." She shook her head. "No, really, you go on without me."

"You can't help them from here," he said. "Maybe—maybe—from Germany." He pulled her arm as a family with small children scurried past them toward a bluish train backing into platform one.

She stiffened. "*Provyerka dokumentov!*" (Review of documents!) A last Russian inspection before boarding. She glanced into her compact mirror, and clicked it shut. A final eye-to-eye exchange, again, that hint of a smile; as if fellow Slavs, Ukrainians, and Russians infallibly recognized each other.

The office of resettlement had provided the Stemmler couple with two seats in what the Germans called *Holzklasse* (wood class). Theo watched the remaining overhead bins fill up with wooden suitcases and cloth bags. Most of their new fellow passengers looked like oddities from another century, a living museum of polka dots and antique beards. Theo wondered what calamities these refugees were escaping; weather-creased faces of older men; thin-lipped women, surrendering their girlish bloom for a kind of leathery honesty. A girl in a flower-print dress stared back at Theo, just as curiously.

141

Steffie clutched her beads as if the rosary could press the immense locomotive piston rods into motion. "How fast can this go?" she whispered.

"Sixty or seventy kilometers an hour," Theo guessed.

"And how many kilometers to Germany?"

"Maybe six or seven hundred."

The train inched off. Steffie lurched toward the window to watch the faces slide past; then, picking up speed, past those Red Army uniforms, then the rows of double-fluted iron columns, and the empty newspaper kiosks—all gliding away—and finally past the last pot of mountain flowers that once cheered the station—their station. The train accelerated into the darkness, toward some mountain passes, toward an unknown country. "Maybe you're right." She sighed. "Maybe we can help our families from Germany."

Theo wondered how much longer the Wozniaks would survive the Soviet machine, before the commissar came to settle scores with her father and with her brother Vlodko. It took just one malicious neighbor to betray a priest in hiding. And Viktor—how much more would that poor devil have to go through?

He wondered if his luck would hold out, or did some boomerang await them at the border? Slavko had mentioned an agreement—or was it a rumor? — that the Germans and the Russians were swapping escaping Ukrainian nationalists for German Communists escaping the other way. Oh Lord, would these two supposed allies really betray their own citizens so easily? What kind of a supposed anti-Communist Germany would align itself with Stalin's homicidal empire? How long could that partnership last? Theo resolved to stay alert, to avoid casual conversation.

He watched the reddish-bearded father across the aisle from him press his hands together. His clan immediately bowed and began praying—praying as forthrightly as if pausing in a plowed field—their sonorous syllables filling the carriage; but not in any language Theo could identify. He eavesdropped until he recognized a sentence: "*Gev uns dis Tag uns tagliks Brod*" (Give us this day our daily bread). But it sounded like . . . like a slurred form of German. Then he understood— Mennonites, German Mennonites. He remembered them from his history classes. Centuries ago, the Russian Empress Catherine had invited this pacifist Christian sect to settle in colonies throughout eastern Ukraine and up to the Volga, to enable her own backward subjects to learn from these clever and diligent Germans. The Mennonites not only took root but flourished in the semi-arid steppes. Were these migrants returning to their long-lost *Vaterland*, Theo wondered – as part of some population exchange agreement?

At "amen," the Mennonite mother uncovered a wicker basket. Theo hadn't eaten in thirty-six hours, and their ration cards were useless until Germany. He watched her bluish knobby hand pass out eggs, sausage, and what looked like moist poppy-seed bread. The mother looked up and said in their dialect, "*Wat eten met uns?*" and held out a potato roll. Theo swallowed hard and spoke in High German. Due to his wife's morning sickness, the rich food might not agree—

"It'll agree!" Steffie interrupted, snatching the dish and biting through half a potato roll.

The little girl pointed and giggled, swinging her feet. "I know where babies come from," she said.

"Let her eat in peace," her father interjected, and turned to Theo. "You two must have been in quite a hurry to leave Kalush, not even packing food for the trip."

"How long have *you* been travelling?" Theo asked.

The father leaned in. "In a way, we're running, too," he confided. "We've left everything—our farms, our community, our churches." Theo watched the Mennonite girls resume their knitting.

"Ja," a Mennonite woman chimed in. "But the Lord will provide."

The Mennonite man nodded and added, "We prayed and foresaw misfortune. If war comes, the Reds will banish us from the steppes to Kazakhstan, or even Siberia – and take our land."

"But if Stalin—the Lord protect him—only knew what the people below him were planning," the woman said, "he'd put a stop to their scheming. Just like that!" She broke a pretzel and gave each son a half.

"We're returning to Germany now," her husband said. "But we know that generations ago, the kaiser exiled our forefathers because they refused to fight in his wars." His eyes lingered on the two boys of military age across from him. "And now the Lord will test our commitment again." He stared at his lacerated boots for a moment. "We will remain true to our covenant, even in this new Germany, even with this new kaiser, who calls himself a Führer."

"Did you understand the gist?" Theo whispered in Ukrainian.

Steffie looked away. "I just sense that they're good people."

Just before midnight, the train stopped at Rzeszow, where fifteen weeks earlier, Roman Catholic priests had flung holy water at Theo's passing infantry unit as they quick-marched toward their rendezvous with catastrophe. He realized that he hadn't yet notified his father or his sisters of his escape. Was it already too late to get word to Hadynkivtsi? The Kalush NKVD may have already directed their Chortkiv colleagues to arrest his family there. Or, he hoped, maybe the NKVD had bigger fish to fry. Ah! The thorough Soviet killing machine. He visualized the gears turning and grinding through human gristle . . . and suddenly felt a terminal exhaustion, like the night he'd spent in the open fields after his capture.

Outside, the snow drifted and darted with the wind, as if to accompany the rhythm of the rails. Theo lost himself in the swirl, closed his eyes, and drifted back, letting the blizzard's white dance carry him back along the tracks.

Each ka-lack, ka-lack . . . ka-lack, ka-lack of the rails propelled him farther back to Kalush, the fields and the stations reappearing and blurring along the hundreds of kilometers; back to his lonely street, to his brooding building, back inside his deathly still apartment, so much like the snowed-in cottage of his youth, the deathly still snowed-in cottage, where he stood motionless, waiting for his appointment. And he never missed an appointment. He heard the knocking, the hard, incessant demand of a fist against the door. They'd come for him, just as Moskalenko said they would.

He opened his eyes and saw the Mennonites awake and focused on the door, which swung open. "Passkontrolle," he heard the German phrase for the first time. They'd arrived in the Polish town of Kielce, the demarcation between the Russian and German zones of occupied Poland, ironically famous for Pilsudski's first campaign for Polish independence. Theo glanced at his watch. It was just after two in the morning—the NKVD's witching hour. They'd be searching the abandoned apartment now. He welcomed Steffie's cheek pressed against his chest, a heavy sleeper who just slurred whatever came into her head when awakened. "Back in Kalush already?" she murmured. "What do you want for breakfast?" He shushed her, gently squeezed her shoulder with one hand, and pulled the passport with the *Reisebescheinigung* out of his inner coat pocket. With a perfunctory salute, the German control officer accepted them as fellow Germans.

ACKNOWLEDGEMENT

I wish to thank my immediate and extended family for responding to my endless requests to revisit their memory banks, their boxes of old letters and family archives and to help me examine a string of implausible but nevertheless true incidents from the war. I am particularly indebted to my immediate family for reviewing a seemingly interminable stream of drafts. I extend a special thanks to my son Alex, especially for his knack for finding just the right detail or character insight to bring a scene fully to life.